PRAISE FOR *VILE*

"Rebecca Jones-Howe's *Vile Men* is an exciting, dark, sexy collection that is convulsively beautiful and bright. Each story digs a great hole and is filled with the most savage, brutal, human emotions: love, desire, addiction and the impossibility of satisfaction."

—ANTONIA CRANE, author of *Spent*

"Rebecca Jones-Howe fearlessly tackles the ugliness most of us manage to hide. Each broken character blurs the lines between villain and victim as they bathe in sex, horror, dignity, want, resignation, and darkness. *Vile Men* is the handbook to uncovering your damage."

—MERCEDES M. YARDLEY, author of *Pretty Little Dead Girls*

"Rebecca Jones-Howe takes you on a tour of the human psyche that is dark, disturbing, and exquisitely written. The sentences in this book are the best kind of dangerous. Just when you think you're safe another one comes along and draws blood."

—ROB HART, author of *New Yorked*

"Rebecca Jones-Howe's *Vile Men* shows us characters driven by desperation to do violence to themselves or others, but behind these sharp stories about the horror of gender and sex is an empathetic insight into human weakness. Jones-Howe might bring us to the darkest parts of the human heart, but her stories remind us that we are all a little bit vile, too."

—LETITIA TRENT, author of *Echo Lake*

"*Vile Men* is dark, provocative stuff. The men found within these pages are indeed bad news, but the most dangerous paths aren't always led by them, as Rebecca Jones-Howe's narrators take us right past the expected awfulness of dead-end, drug-addled relationships, bad sex on ant hills, or navigating the treacherous rubble of the bar scene, where her women can find satisfaction and even surprise flashes of triumph amongst all the emotional jetsam. 'There's a certain kind of man who goes for damaged girls,' she writes. They may be broken, but as vile as these men may be (and always such needy little beasts) they don't get to have everything."

—DAVID JAMES KEATON, author of *The Last Projector*

REBECCA JONES-HOWE

VILE MEN

PUBLISHED BY DARK HOUSE PRESS, AN IMPRINT OF
CURBSIDE SPLENDOR PUBLISHING, INC., CHICAGO, ILLINOIS IN 2015.

FIRST EDITION
COPYRIGHT © 2015 BY REBECCA JONES-HOWE
LIBRARY OF CONGRESS CONTROL NUMBER: 2015943880
ISBN 978-1-94-043051-5

EDITED BY RICHARD THOMAS
DESIGNED BY ALBAN FISCHER

MANUFACTURED IN THE UNITED STATES OF AMERICA.
WWW.THEDARKHOUSEPRESS.COM

To my high school drafting teacher, Mr. Bouwman.
You always said that I would dedicate my first book to you,
so here you go.

CONTENTS

VILE MEN

HONEY BADGERS
WILL EAT
PRACTICALLY
ANYTHING.

He grunts and pulls me toward him. I slip over the counter, tightening my fingers around its squared edge. He grips my waist, slides his hand down. He grabs my ass and pushes himself into me.

The moan I make is legit.

"Am I a real princess?" I ask.

He slaps my tits.

I don't sound like Kate Middleton, but he fucks me like I'm a princess. He digs deep, buries his nails into my thighs. His breath catches, the sound filling the room with desperation and exhaustion.

I'm grateful that I can't see his expression from behind the paper bag.

"Fuck," he says. "Fuck, fuck, fuck."

This is probably how he masturbates when he's alone, all of his aggression and anger and frustration in a crescendo of solitary release. He comes before I can, but his taut grasp burns a release through my limbs. He slips over me. His chest beats against my stomach. He gasps for breath and then he groans and lets me go.

He pulls off the paper bag and I'm fixed again.

I press my back against the mirror. Goosebumps form on my flushed skin. I reach up and rub the back of my neck, drawing a breath of cold bathroom air. He's already turned around, his back to me.

"Did you like that?" I ask.

"That was fucked up." He yanks the condom off, his shoulders already tightened, already pretending. "I can't believe you do this shit," he says.

"Was it like fucking a princess?" I ask.

"No." He tosses the rubber in the garbage and then bends down to pick up his pants.

"That's too bad," I say, "because you made me feel like one."

He crumples up the paper bag, crumples Kate's face. He throws the bag at me and he does up his pants, buckles his belt. His eyes dart up at me as adjusts his shirt.

Honey Badger Don't Care.

"You totally care," I say.

"What?" he asks.

I point at his chest. "You're wearing that ironically, right?"

He looks down at the badger and then back at me.

"It's okay," I say. "We're all human, right?"

"Fuck you," he says. The door closes behind him and I'm left alone again.

His beer's still beside me on the counter. I bring the bottle to my lips. The dregs are warm and awful, but the last of my endorphin rush makes the taste almost tolerable.

I slip off the counter and pick the paper bag off the floor. I smooth out the lines on Kate's face. She's not really a princess but everybody likes to pretend she is. She mirrors my smile and I fold her nicely before slipping her back into my purse.

I've kept every single paper bag I've ever worn.

EVERY CLIMB UP TO
HIS BEDROOM
MAKES ME FEEL LIKE
I'M STARTING OVER.

BLUE HAWAII

The jogging stroller squeaks to the time of my sloppy pace up the hill. My calves ache, and all I can think of is relief, the sound of rum rushing from the bottle to a glass. Distraction. It's the sort of thought that jogging can't push away.

Every run uphill makes me feel like I'm starting over.

The dry summer parches its way down my throat, making every exhale a cough. I wipe at the sweat on my face, smearing the cover-up above my lip.

"Shit."

The baby starts crying. Leaning over the handle of the stroller, I reach out and touch her cheek. Her eyes close into tight wrinkles and her mouth gapes wide. Her screeches fill my ears.

"Please stop," I gasp.

She doesn't. I turn the stroller around and walk back to my sister's townhouse. The baby's wails force me to shut my eyes. Even the speed bump at the complex entrance feels like a burden.

"Hey, there. Hey!" It's a male voice calling.

I turn around and the new neighbour jogs past.

"Hey," he says again. He's wearing a navy blue shirt and white jogging shorts. A sweatband pushes his brown hair back. "You okay?" he asks, running in place. "You don't look so great. You look beat. You're probably dehydrated."

He's tall, lean, with a pale face and a beard. His pupils are dilated, but I can still see that his eyes are the colour of a Blue Hawaii, the first drink I ever had. All I can think of is the chilled pineapple sweetness as my gaze trickles down. He's sweating, and the fabric of his shirt clings to his chest.

My fingers tense around the stroller.

He takes a drink from his water bottle, and then rotates it in his grasp so the water clings to the sides. "You live just over there, right?" he asks, pointing. "I know because I saw you. You were in the window with that other girl. You were watching me move all my shit."

"That was my sister, Marie," I say. "I live with her and her baby."

"You should come in," he says, paying no attention to the crying infant in the stroller. "You're not busy, right? I can show you my place."

"I don't know," I say.

"Come on." He jogs backwards, his smile too nice, eyes so intense like Blue Hawaii vacation excitement. "Come on," he urges. "You can have a glass of water. I promise I'll make it cold and refreshing. I promise. I guarantee, even."

———

THERE'S AN ANT'S NEST beside his front door, a swarm of black crawling around my feet. Inside, his place is barren, the boxes still taped up, stacked beside his kitchen counter. There's a couch in the living room. The suede clings to the sweat on my thighs when I sit down.

He gets me a glass of water and sits beside me. He watches me drink. "You had a cleft lip," he says.

"What?"

"You did at one point, didn't you?" He rubs at his nose, sniffing. "I mean, it doesn't look like it, but I can see the scar."

My hand flinches, touching the uneven skin. He catches my wrist, his palm hot, sweaty. I jerk my hand away.

"I'm sorry," he says. He laughs, leaning forward, unable to sit still.

"I've seen all those pictures of babies with cleft lips. It's crazy that those kids can look so normal, isn't it?"

"I guess," I say. The scar throbs and I stare down at the floor. I flinch, thinking of the ants on the doorstep, crawling around my feet like early memories: learning to speak without slurring, trying to explain to classmates why my mouth was so ugly, all that social withdrawal sewn up inside my restructured upper lip. It's hard to breathe. I turn my head and take a drink. The water's cold but it doesn't provide the right kind of relief.

"Do you want to do something?" He edges closer, his hands shaking, fingers brushing against my leg. "Do you want to fuck?"

My grasp tightens around the glass.

"Sex is just the best when I'm high," he says. "It feels so fucking good."

I brace myself when he slides his hand up my thigh. "What are you high on?" I ask.

His lips curl into a smile. "It's coke," he says. "It makes me want to fuck you so fucking hard." He fingers at the leg of my shorts, pinching the fabric.

My gaze drifts to the baby, now asleep. Her head's slumped forward. Her eyes are closed and her mucus-filled nose makes sounds every time she breathes in and out—dazed, dreaming.

He leans in—the sweet scent of his cologne mixed with perspiration, something new, something worth trying. I set the glass down on the floor. "You have to be quiet," I say. "You can't wake her, okay?"

He's got a face beyond my league, but he kisses me, eager. His tongue probes past the scar. Warmth settles between my legs. My limbs loosen. My veins run hot, heart throbbing, and I sink back, giving in. This is what everything used to feel like when I first started drinking. No tension, just a black hole to fill with anything.

"My name's Ian," he says, climbing over me on the couch. He stares me down, his big eyes just dark holes with blue edges. He's somewhere else, somewhere better. He kisses me again, thick saliva in my throat, taking me with him.

He pries at my clothes, his hands quick, aggressive. He pulls his shorts down and grabs my knees, shoving his dick between my legs. "You're so fucking wet," he says. "You fucking like me, don't you? You fucking want me, don't you, baby?"

He wakes the baby. Her cries squeal like the stroller wheels.

I shut my eyes and smooth my palms over his chest, feeling the rapid pace, the pulsing throbs. Under him, everything else is hard to hear.

———

When Marie comes home from work, I sit up straight on the couch, holding the baby, pretending there's nothing to hide.

"I met the new neighbour today," I say.

"Oh yeah?" She sets her purse down on the table.

"His name's Ian. He's really nice. He showed me his place."

She looks at me. My lip itches and I rub it with the back of my hand. I can still smell the sweat on my skin.

"How was Emma today?" she asks, taking the baby.

"Fussy," I say. "I don't think she likes jogging, the motion of it. I don't think it does anything for her."

———

At night Ian follows me. He chases me through the dirt trail beside the highway. The sun beats down on my skin. I can barely run, and he tackles me into the sagebrush, the gravel scraping at my flesh. There's an ant's nest beside my face.

"What did your mouth look like?" he asks.

"I don't remember," I say. "My mom never took pictures of me."

"It was probably a hole you could slip right into," he says, his voice hot and eager in my ear. He slides two fingers into the nest and the ants crawl out. I realize he's naked, that I'm naked. I wince, arching myself against his hard-on. He enters me, invades me, and I gasp, the ants finding a new home in my mouth, crawling inside.

I wake up in my bedroom. There's nothing but black outside the tiny window, and I lay there, looking at the shadows, the comfort of them.

I PUT THE BABY in the stroller, her little mouth filled with a pacifier so she's quiet, non-existent. I walk across the parking lot and knock on Ian's door. He's shaved off his beard and his face is marked with little red nicks. His skin looks sallow. He stares with empty blue eyes. There's a plastic bottle of white powder clutched in his hand.

I push the stroller inside and lean against the door.

"I just want to do another line," he says. "That's all I ever want to do. That's all I can think about." His voice is low, quiet, the way mine used to sound when going out stopped being about blended drinks and partying, when it was solely about the alcohol, its influence feeding my veins.

"It's better to talk than to keep it all in," I say.

"What does it matter to you?"

"I was an alcoholic," I say.

He stares.

"It's still hard, trying not to think about it, knowing it's not an option. I told myself I didn't want it to be an option. It just makes everything even harder." My gaze drops. I step forward, breathing in, inhaling the scent of him.

His fingers curl around the bottle. "It's getting worse," he says. "The first time I did it, I felt like angels were in the walls. They were talking to me, giving me energy and powers. Now the highs never last as long, and when I come down I just, I can't even do anything."

"Do you ever think of hurting yourself?" I ask.

He shakes his head.

My lip twitches. He watches me rub at the scar. "I tried to cut it open once," I say. "Marie found me in the bathroom with a knife. I told her there was nowhere else for the bullshit to go. The hole had to get bigger. All she did was cry. She didn't know what to say. Nobody ever did."

His hand starts shaking. The bottle looks like a tiny martini shaker in his grasp, the powder inside like white drink froth.

"There's no point taking it out on yourself," I say. "It's better when you're not alone."

He pours a bump on his wrist and he snorts it back. His chest heaves in and out. He looks at me, his lips tight, eyes wide, hot. He smiles. Blue Hawaii vacation relief.

I want it. I want him.

———

MARIE WAKES ME UP, walking into my bedroom with the baby wailing in her arms. "Where's Emma's pacifier?" she asks. "You had it this morning. She can't fall asleep without it."

"I don't know," I say. "Maybe it fell out at Ian's place."

"What?" Her face is blurry in the dark. "You went there again?"

"I was talking with him. What's wrong with that?"

"You're supposed to be looking after Emma," she says.

"I get bored sometimes," I say. "What do you expect, that I'm just going to sit and listen to her cry all day?"

Marie groans. "I thought you were done with all this," she says. "You can take care of yourself now. Why can't you help somebody else?" She slams the door, but it doesn't mask the sound of the baby's colic moans.

———

IAN NEVER UNPACKS. He tells me that he's started selling his stuff to pay for more cocaine. He's so high, so excited, stubble on his face. He lets his beard grow back.

I buy pacifiers. There's a bag of them on his kitchen counter. The baby cries and I pop one in. Her mouth is so pretty, so perfect. Her lips close around the pacifier and she falls asleep like a normal person. Then Ian does another line.

Every climb up to his bedroom makes me feel like I'm starting over.

Blue Hawaii vacation refreshment.

———

HE DOESN'T HAVE A BED. There's just a mattress on the floor, and it squeaks like the baby's stroller when he fucks me on it. He's shaved again. The scabs are thick, dark, like ants are crawling on his face. His nostrils are lined in red.

The room smells like sweat and bile and aftermath. Sickness. His dick slips in, and he goes hard, fast, deep, filling me until my stomach cramps. His groan echoes when he pulls out, gushing hot all over my torso. He rubs his hands over the sticky white, slides two fingers into my mouth, making me taste him.

"Don't you like me?" he asks. "Don't you want me?"

He pries my lip up, pinching right where the scar is. "What's it like, knowing you were born with all the ugly on the outside?"

It feels like ants are crawling in my veins.

"It used to be so different," he says, voice cracking.

I wince, but I can't shake him off. He clings to me, nails bearing into my skin like tiny bites that sting all over. His groan echoes, turns into a moan. My lip throbs.

"It's never like it used to be," he says, his eyes turning red, blinking, tears slipping out. It's like a Blue Hawaii vacation gone awry.

He's on his hands and knees, shoulders shaking. His sobs sound stuck in his throat. It's how my cries must have sounded when I was a baby, when my mouth was still a gaping open mess. I crawl away from him, his sweetness diluted on my tongue.

———

I hold my breath, standing at the living room window. The baby's crying in my arms and I rock her, watching Ian as he bends down over his doorstep, an aerosol can of insect killer clutched in his unsteady hand.

Marie comes home.

"Jessica, are you okay?"

I shake my head, my fingers flinching, the baby slipping. Marie takes her, pats her back. She looks out the window.

"I'm sorry," I say. My fingers clench but there's nothing to hold onto. "I relapsed."

Marie looks at me.

"I'm not going back there. I just wanted to feel like I used to."

"What is going on?" she asks.

I shake my head, tight-lipped. Outside, Ian turns, looking up at the window, at me, nothing but black filling his gaze. I look away.

———

EMMA WAKES ME, crying again. There's blue behind the white sheer of the curtains. Dawn. Marie's in the living room, trying to soothe the baby back to sleep. She doesn't notice me.

"I can take her," I say.

"Huh?" Marie blinks, looking up.

"Go to bed," I say. "I can take her for you."

Emma settles in my arms, her cries fading. Her skin's warm and soft, her tiny infant grasp clinging to my finger. In the daylight, her eyes glisten bright blue. Normal.

HIS SMILE IS A TICKET
TO FRANCE BUT I KNOW
THE TRUTH,   THAT UNDER
THE EIFFEL TOWER
IS JUST A BUNCH OF
HOMELESS PEOPLE.

TOURIST

There's a certain kind of man who goes for damaged girls. He does the double take when he spots me from across the room. He spies the filtered grey that clouds my gaze and he doesn't look away. A man like that is a travel magazine in a hospital waiting room. You could go anywhere, see anything, but you'd never want to waste the money. Still, he stares. He smiles lightly. My chest tingles and I want to breathe in deep.

The things I'd do if I could, but I know better.

I always run.

———

JESSA AND HER HUSBAND are trying to conceive a child. I hear them sometimes, the sound of the headboard hitting the wall, their voices moaning. There's a picture of a beach above my desk and when I squint my eyes I can see the frame bobbing. Hearing them makes me wonder what will happen to me.

Their condominium only has two bedrooms.

Jessa says she wants a girl. I think about a girl lying where I am now on the floor, in the room where she'll become herself. I wonder what kind of pictures she'll put up. Most girls hang pictures of boys and pretty pop stars, the things they want and things they hope to be.

I wonder if she'll be more like me.

My parents were told they were going to have a boy but when I came out female they never bothered to repaint the walls. I remember asking my dad for a white bedroom that looked like the hotel rooms in the travel magazines at the doctor's office.

"You're just going to get everything dirty," he said.

I remember crying. I remember him putting his arms around me. He said that little girls weren't supposed to have white bedrooms and it made me feel like I'd done something wrong. He repeated it over and over while he wiped the tears on my cheeks. I wanted to fight. I wanted to kick and scream but I didn't.

My girlhood walls remained barren and slate blue.

———

MOST PEOPLE APPEAR to be absent when they fall under the spell of routine, their faces bleached with a sullen sense of sadness as their bodies drift from place to place. He walks into the coffee shop with a placid expression. He orders his coffee and waits at the counter, his gaze distant, connecting with nothing.

Then he notices me.

I sit up in my seat. My fingers clench but there's nothing to hold onto.

The barista gives him his coffee in a disposable cup. He's a man on the go. He's older, because they always are. He approaches like they all do. His smile is a ticket to France, but I know the truth, that under the Eiffel Tower is just a bunch of homeless people.

"You were here the other day," he says, setting his coffee down. "Same table."

I bite my lip and raise my chin. My throat tenses and then I remember his face, his square jawline, his chin shadowed with stubble. He's going to sit but he doesn't yet. He drums his fingers over the plastic lid of his coffee cup. I meet his warm gaze. He has a real man's smile. It's first class.

I'm supposed to nod, so I do. In my head I'm frantic. I'm packing, trying to prepare.

I tug at my white blouse. The fabric's rough. It's been bleached so much it almost looks yellow. Discoloured. He unbuttons his wool coat as he sits down and I can't help but feel under-dressed.

"Do you come here every day?" he asks.

"Before work," I say, already breathless. "It's somewhere to go. I'm supposed to have some time out, time to myself." It's something my therapist used to say.

"You don't really look like you're enjoying it," he says.

"My coffee's still hot," I say.

He looks down at the ceramic mug in my hands. My fingers twitch over the handle. My chest goes tight and I draw a breath, curling my toes. I try not to run.

"What's your name?" he asks.

"Angie." It's starting, the turbine engine in my ears.

"Short for Angela?" he asks.

"I just go by Angie."

"Okay," he says. "Angie." He pulls his chair closer, shoulders hunched as he leans in.

I want to pull away. I want to put my head between my knees. I want to kick and scream but I don't. All I can do is breathe.

Inhale, exhale. It's a routine.

⸻

I ALWAYS WANTED to be a road map, a girl who danced on a table and then let all the men explore. Behind closed doors, opening up, they'd become a piece of land to conquer. Girls like that have the allure of Las Vegas. It's the same thing every time but men always want to go back. What happens there stays there.

I'm more like a guided tour. I give a hint, a glimpse, but then a man tries to push past the blue velvet. He runs his hand up my thigh and I grab his palm with shaking fingers.

All he gets is a chance to snap a photo that looks worse than the one in the travel guide.

———

Jessa's been rubbing circles over her stomach ever since the test she bought came out positive. Her stomach's flat and normal, but she still comforts the hidden life inside while we sit in her doctor's waiting room. She says she's nervous and I tell her I'm nervous *for* her, even though I know that's not what friends are supposed to say. There's a stack of magazines on the waiting room table. The one on the top is called *Destinations*. There's a picture of a French vineyard on the cover.

I think about telling Jessa my big news. She holds my hand, her fingers tight, the only grasp I can trust. She flinches when she's called in.

"I'm so excited," she says.

"I thought you were nervous," I say.

Everybody in the waiting room looks up. They look at me and not at Jessa. They look at me like I'm lost. Jessa asks if I want to go with her, but I shake my head and stay in my cold plastic seat. I pick up the travel magazine and flip through the pages. I rub at my stomach, nothing inside but an ache that builds, as I look at all the glossy pictures—all the places I'll never visit.

———

He calls in the night, his name darkening the picture of the vineyard on my phone:

FRANCIS

"Hey, Angie."

The beach on my wall is shaking again. Now that Jessa and her husband aren't trying, they're making love. Their moans still sound the same. I pull the covers over my head and shield myself with the darkness and the silence, save for his voice in my ear.

"This a bad time?" he asks.

I shake my head even though he can't see me, the weight of the duvet bearing down on top of me. I clear my throat. "I'm okay," I say.

"Do most men wait a week before they call you?"

"No," I say before swallowing. "I don't know."

He laughs gently. He's not mocking, but I feel mocked.

He asks me how work was. He asks, "What's your favourite kind of bread to make?"

"I don't know."

"Sure you do," he says.

I hesitate. "I like cinnamon buns, the kind with the raisins."

"I should come in and buy one, right?"

"Maybe," I say.

"How about we get one right now?"

"The bakery's closed," I say.

"We'll go somewhere else," he says. "Somewhere open."

I can hear Jessa's husband, his grunts echoing. I pull the covers tighter around me. I don't ever want to leave.

"You up for that?" he asks.

I'm not, but I have to be.

———

I walk with heavy steps, the heels of my Mary Janes hitting the pavement, sounding like the headboard against the wall.

Trying, trying, trying.

The sound becomes comforting, hard throbs filling empty streets, echoing skyward. I pull my coat around me to recreate the effect of the duvet, of my bedroom. There are no stars above, just black like the ceiling.

My steps echo across the parking lot. The only place open is the grocery store he wanted to meet me at. I sit on the bench outside and wait. It's like waiting for Jessa's doctor to call her in, only without the travel magazines.

He pulls up in his Accord. It's blue like my bedroom walls.

"You haven't been waiting long, have you?" he asks.

I shake my head and he walks up, puts his hand on my back to guide me into the store. The only cinnamon buns come packaged as a pre-sliced doughy rectangle of six in a flimsy plastic container. They aren't pretty like the fresh ones at the bakery. They're slathered thick with icing, but he buys them and we sit outside on the bench, the container between us. He picks out a bun, and peels at the coiled dough.

"This is different," he says.

"Yeah," I say. My shoes click against the pavement as my legs swing back and forth, and I catch him looking down, his gaze tracing over the definition of my calves under white tights.

"I always pick up coffee on the way to work," he says. "You're always there. I didn't think I'd ever talk to you until you actually looked up. I was going to the other day, but then you stood up and ran off."

I reach for a cinnamon bun, the icing sticking to my fingers. They're shaking, so I put the bun back down. I clear my throat. "It's the only place I ever go aside from work," I say, bringing my fingers to my lips. The icing is sweet, reacting to my tongue.

"Do you live alone?" he asks.

"I live with my friend," I say. "She's married. They own a condo but it's tiny. Sometimes I feel like I'm going insane." My chest tenses like it always does when I get too close. I don't know why I'm saying everything, but it comes out like I'm still sitting in front of my therapist, a life's worth of burdens needing relief.

"You should get your own place," he says.

"I had my own apartment before." I bite my lip but the taste of the icing is gone. "I couldn't really afford it," I say. My fingers grasp around the edge of the bench.

His gaze drops. He notices.

"You're a careful girl, aren't you?" he asks.

My lips tighten and I glance at the cinnamon bun I can't eat.

"You take your time," he says.

I take a breath, glancing down at the pavement, at my shoes.

"It's okay," he says. "I won't push you."

He puts his hand over mine and I flinch. His hand's warm, his grip soft. I can't help but draw a breath. The way his fingers twitch, I know he wants to go everywhere.

I wonder how long he'll wait.

———

I DREAM OF MY FATHER. I'm six years old but I'm fully grown, and I walk downstairs and find him watching television with the lights off. He's watching his secret movies again. His fist is gripped, pumping over his lap. His movies are always the same but with different girls in different classrooms.

This time a girl in a blue uniform is getting spanked over her desk.

"You're a dirty girl, aren't you?" her teacher asks before unzipping his pants. He slips his hand under her shirt and he gropes her breasts.

The girl nods, her pigtails bobbing.

Heat fills my throat. I want to run but my legs don't move. I cry instead, scared and lost in my own home. Dad turns around, his shadow shifting in the dark. He gets out of his chair. He covers my face. His hand is sticky, smelling of salt water.

I wake with the memory of Mom's voice in my ear. She's angry, yelling, "You've ruined her, you know that?"

———

THE NURSE PUTS the wand over Jessa's stomach and I look up at the screen, trying to find her baby, lost somewhere in the static. I'm holding Jessa's hand and I force myself to think it's like holding Francis' hand but it's not. Jessa's palm is soft and she clings tight like she's holding me, guarding me, keeping me safe.

Like always.

But then the nurse tells Jessa that the stormy blur on the screen is a girl and Jessa lets me go. She covers her mouth. Her eyes tear up and she looks at me.

"I've always wanted a girl," she says.

The screen whirs. I take a breath but the air feels thick. I can hear the ocean.

THE OVERCAST SKY is easy to look at, low-hanging grey clouds stretched like a bedroom ceiling all the way to work. I order my coffee just like Francis, and the barista gives me the to-go cup with the plastic lid. I carry it to work with me. The heat seeps through the flimsy waxed cardboard, warming my palm.

I walk past a mother holding her daughter's hand. The girl tilts her head to look at me. She makes eye contact. She looks afraid. The mother looks Jessa's age but she looks so much older than me. She smiles and says, "Hello."

I forget to answer because I'm still looking at the girl, at the fear in her gaze.

The mother pulls the girl past me and the girl turns her head. She stares.

I never identify with mothers.

THERE ARE THINGS a girl needs to know. Mom told me those things when I first started talking about the boys in my class. Those boys seemed less interesting the more Mom told me about how they would become men. That was what she always called them. *Men.*

"It's when his gaze looks different than it did before," she said. "That's when you have to ask yourself what he really wants."

Tour guides know everything.

But I don't.

I don't know what to say when Francis surprises me, when he walks into the bakery. He waits in line, his gaze directed at the cinnamon buns behind the counter. I ask him what he wants but he doesn't buy anything. He looks up and asks me when I'm off work.

I want to go home, to lie under my duvet. It's hard to not want that with him standing in front of the counter, the last customer in the store, ten minutes before closing.

"You don't have any plans, do you?" he asks. He stares at me like he knows me.

I shake my head and take off my apron. I run my shaking fingers down my bleached white shirt. It's dirty, stiff, and gritty.

When I close the store he offers me his arm. I link mine through and he bends his elbow, pulls me against him. He smells like the candle in my bedroom, the welcome gift Jessa and her husband gave when I first moved into their spare bedroom. I never lit it because it smelled so masculine, so foreign. The scent was printed on the side of the box.

Coastal Boardwalk.

HE TAKES ME BACK to the coffee shop. We sit face to face and I feel familiar enough to ask him where he works. He says he works at the post office, sorting mail." It pays okay," he says. "It's just not the sort of place you enjoy working. You know the things they say about postal workers? Some of them are true."

I look at him.

"Everybody eats their lunch in their car."

"Do you?" I ask.

"Sometimes," he says, pulling off the end of his cinnamon bun." Sometimes I go out. Maybe I'll come visit you instead."

I want to ask him what he likes about me but I can't. All I hear is Mom's uncertain voice telling me what sex was after I asked her about the schoolgirls in Dad's movies.

"It's what grown-ups do," she said. "They do it when they're in love."

Francis smiles in front of me. I feel another twitch in my chest. It makes me think of the ocean. I take a sip of coffee but all I taste is salt in my mouth.

JESSA SITS ON MY BED rubbing lotion on her stomach, her massaged slow circles now routine. She doesn't wear makeup anymore, despite always worrying about how she looks. She says she's too tired to really care. She sounds like she knows what she's talking about. She smiles as she pushes gently on the bump the baby's made. It's a small bump, but I can see it.

"It's stiff," she says. "It feels so weird."

She takes my hand and places it over her belly. I push down, feeling the hardness. The bump almost looks like an infection, the manifestation of her love for her husband. It's ruining her figure.

She looks at me. The little crow's feet that creep from her eyes look like Mom's.

"Who was that man who dropped you off the other day?"

That word again. *Man*. It makes him seem so distant.

"His name's Francis," I say.

"Oh?" she asks, her lips curving. "You met a man named Francis, hey?"

I nod.

"What's he like?" she asks.

"He's nice," I say. I picture him eating lunch in his car and my chest warms like the sun's touching it. My cheeks flush.

"He's not like the other men?" she asks.

I shake my head. "He likes to talk," I say.

"What do you talk about?"

Jessa never asks questions, but they come one after the other. I think of when Jessa first met her husband and I nervously asked her for every detail. She knew everything and I didn't, but now I tell her about the first day Francis saw me at the coffee shop and I was too scared to stay. I tell her about the day he approached, how I could have run but I didn't. I tell her about the cinnamon buns. I tell her about the Boardwalk. It's the most I've spoken in weeks.

"I remember buying you that candle," she says. "I didn't know you still had it. I thought you hated it."

"I wasn't used to it back then."

Jessa kisses me on the forehead. "I like seeing you like this," she says.

I REMEMBER FINDING Dad's stash of movies in the shoebox where his formal shoes should have been. It was like getting lost, a foreign country, just pictures of women in girls' clothing, shirts cut low and skirts hitched up. I showed Mom because I wanted to know why she never dressed like that.

She used to know everything.

Her crow's feet deepened when she opened the box. Her lips pursed. She looked angry and she was supposed to be in love.

It was their seventh anniversary. They were supposed to go out for dinner, but Mom took the box of movies and threw it in Dad's face.

"Where are your goddamn shoes?" she asked.

"MY PARENTS DIVORCED when I was ten," I say, looking down at my shoes, running them over the mat in his car. "I lived with my mom and I saw my dad on weekends."

"Did it bother you?" he asked.

"I don't know," I say. "My best friend's parents divorced when she was a kid, but she was younger. She handled it better than I did."

I think of Jessa on her wedding day. Her dad wasn't there, so I walked her down the aisle. She always said I meant just as much to her as she did to me. But it was her hand pulling me along. The wedding was outdoors and it had rained early in the morning, the smell of dirt piercing the field. I couldn't close my eyes during the prayer. My gaze was pinned on the dirt that stained the train of her dress. I wanted to bend down, to clean it off. I wanted to do something for her.

Francis looks at his watch.

"My break's almost over," he says.

I look out the windshield, back at the bakery, at my boss, her gentle pink smile flushed as she arranges the buns behind the glass counter. Francis takes my hand and leans over the space between the seats. He kisses me. His lips are slightly cold but they're soft and sweet, filling me with a warmth that trickles down into my lungs.

I kiss him back, still tasting the icing after he pulls away.

———

I USED TO COLLECT old postcards of France, the same monuments, just different angles, different shades of muted colour—the dog-eared matte paper comforting under my fingers. I used to wonder what people did once they got there, if the romance was real, if the feeling flooded their veins.

"When I hear clicking shoes I think of you," he says, his voice faint over the phone. "I know it's late but I want to see you."

I'm burning my candle, his scent filling the room.

"I want you to come over," he says.

He said he wasn't going to push, but I don't remind him. I look at the candle, the red-hot flame, Las Vegas heat in my lungs. I drop the postcards back into the shoebox that once held my Mary Janes. I tell him to pick me up.

I push the shoebox under the bed just as Jessa walks into the room.

"It smells too manly," she says, leaning back against my bed, pulling herself onto the mattress. She looks at the candle and then at me. I take her feet in my hands and massage the swells.

"How old is he?" she asks.

"He's turning forty," I say.

Her foot twitches in my hand. "Do you really like him?" she asks.

"I can talk to him," I say.

"Do you tell him things about yourself?"

"I don't know," I say. "Small things. I told him about Mom and Dad."

She looks over at the burning candle. "Have you slept with him?"

I shake my head and she looks at her stomach, smoothing her hand over the bump that's bigger now. She knows how long it's been since the last man took me somewhere.

"What do you want from him?" she asks.

I didn't think it was a question I could answer, and I wish she'd tell me what I'm supposed to want, but she grips at her stomach for a moment, shuts her eyes and moans. I want to ask her if she's okay, but I don't know what I'd do if she wasn't.

I think of when she found me in my old apartment, camped out on soiled blankets in the living room, rotting food on the counters, remnants of the weeks I'd spent without leaving. Back then I didn't want to leave. I didn't want to go anywhere, but Jessa came to me and she touched my cheek, the warmth of her palm like sunlight I hadn't felt in days.

She said, "Ang, you're not okay."

Her voice echoes in my head and then I hear Francis' car pull up outside. Jessa exhales slowly, pulling her feet from my lap. She winces again, and rubs at her stomach before she leans over and blows out the candle.

———

HE SITS BESIDE ME on his couch. He's turned to me, looking at me, his gaze like an ocean that goes on forever. I look away. His house is sparse and clean. His kitchen has stainless steel appliances and dark hardwood floors. He has matching leather couches with coordinating cushions. There's a stack of coasters on the coffee table.

I glance at my Mary Janes, kicked off on the floor beside his door.

"Did you ever have boyfriends before?" he asks.

I nod, thinking of the other men, the ones who visited Las Vegas and never wanted to talk about it after.

"I had a boyfriend in high school," I say. I take a drink from the wine he gave me. It's white wine, but it looks more yellow than white in the glass. It goes down dry. He leans in close, his breath full of expectation. I imagine the sound of my feet running on the boardwalk.

"I was sixteen," I say. "He said he wanted to be my first."

Francis runs his fingers over my knee. He's gentle but I can feel the tremors.

"It went how it was supposed to. I was nervous. He took the lead."

"Did you want him to?" Francis asks.

My grasp tightens around the glass. I never thought much to remember it, the face of the boy who first said manly things to me. "I thought I wanted it," I say. "I thought I was supposed to but I didn't really know anything back then."

He leans in. He takes the glass and sets it on the coffee table. No coaster. He slips his hand around my waist and pulls me to him. "I just want to be with you," he says, his voice in my ear again, only this time I can feel the heat of his breath. "I'm in love with you," he says.

He's probably telling the truth.

I know what love sounds like, his shaky breath echoing. He kisses my neck but all I can do is gasp and shudder. He climbs on top of me, his weight heavier than all my blankets and my duvet piled on. His lips cover mine and I picture a beach in an earthquake.

I'm trying. I'm trying.

His touch slips over me. I grip at the cushions on his couch, my grasp getting tighter. I shut my eyes when he undoes the buttons of my blouse. His fingers are cold, the sensation of a wave hitting my chest.

"I don't know anything," I say, the tremors filling my throat, taking over. "I don't know why I came here."

I'm trying. I'm trying.

"Angie." His voice is a soft tremor inside of me. He repeats my name. He asks, "Angie, are you okay?"

Everything feels vast and endless. I clench my toes. My feet are so cold.

He pulls away. He says he's sorry. He says it over and over.

Above me, his ceiling looks like expanding grey sky.

I DREAM THAT FRANCIS AND I try out beds in an endless maze of hotel rooms. He takes my hand and pulls me onto each waiting ensemble. He submerges me under feather pillows and soft covers, but I sink and flail, unable to breathe beneath all the white.

In the morning I wake in my own room, the shame like jet lag as I roll out from under the uneven weight of my duvet.

I put on my work clothes, the blue skirt and bleached shirt, my white tights and Mary Janes. My hair's tied back and I stare at the flickering reflection, feeling like I used to feel when Dad would pick me up from school on Friday afternoons.

In my uniform, I never felt right.

I still don't.

THE ACHE IN MY STOMACH builds, forcing me to leave work early. Jessa doesn't hear me when I kick my shoes off. She's behind her bedroom door with her husband. At first it sounds like they're making love, but then I hear her groan.

"Honey, I can't talk about this. My feet are aching today."

"You have to deal with her eventually," her husband says.

"The baby can stay in our room until she's ready," Jessa says.

"Ready for what?" her husband asks.

"To live on her own."

"Are you serious?" he asks. "She can barely make it to work without falling apart."

"You don't know her like I do," Jessa says, her voice sounding like Mom's. "She goes out all the time."

"To where?" her husband asks.

THE STREETS ARE TURBULENT, my heels clacking on the wet sidewalk. The sky is an infinite span of darkening clouds, stretching over the post office and off to the horizon. I stand in the employee parking lot and wait for him at the side entrance where his co-workers pass in and out, looking just as sad as he once did.

He walks out, keys jangling.

"Angie," he says.

His gaze is on me. It tames the heat of anxiety inside of me. He approaches and I reach up, fingers sliding over his shoulders and around his neck. His coat is long, the buttons undone. The thick wool warms my shoulders when he wraps his arms around me.

"We should go somewhere," he says.

"Your place," I say.

He asks if I'm sure and I nod against his chest, breathing in deep, the scent of the boardwalk.

I'M ON HIS COUCH again, my legs curled underneath me. He sits beside me while I glance outside the living room window at the falling rain.

"What are you so scared of?" he asks.

"I feel like you barely know me at all," I say.

"There's plenty I can see on the surface," he says. It sounds like an insult but it's not. He touches my face, brushes his fingers over my cheek.

I look up at him. I share his gaze. His eyes are blue, like his car.

He's the guide.

"I asked you to spend time with me and you came," he says. "What made you want to?"

I think of my shoes clicking against the sidewalk. I think of my aching calves, of the sky seeming a little less vast when there was somewhere else to go.

"It used to be impossible to go out," I say.

I tell him everything. I tell him about my parents. I tell him about my apartment. I tell him about Jessa, my only girlhood friend who's fading away. He listens. It gets late. He gets me blankets from his linen closet and I fall asleep on the couch. In the morning he's there. We go out for coffee before he drops me off at work.

My clothes are wrinkled, but they feel comfortable, lived-in.

———

JESSA CALLS ME into her bedroom when I get home from work. She's on her bed, circling her stomach with an unsteady palm. She's having contractions—four in under an hour. It's too early. Three months early, she says.

Her hands shake when she grips my wrist.

I think of the baby, no longer contained by the walls of her womb, forced to meet the world too soon.

"It's not supposed to be like this," Jessa says. Her voice cracks.

"You'll be fine," I say. She looks at me, her gaze filled with static and worry like when she found me trapped in my apartment and she cupped my cheek and took me away.

I touch her stomach, my fingers shaking.

"She'll be fine," I say, trying to sound like I know what I'm talking about.

She doesn't look like she believes me.

———

SHE'S A TINY THING, breathing ventilated air, barely moving in the incubator. Looking at her, it's like looking at a picture of a place I've been to.

Jessa's asleep in the sterile room. Her husband's at her side, clutching her pale hand, clutching it tight.

I buy Jessa flowers. They're white lilies and I write on the card, STAY STRONG in big capital letters that look like the text on my phone when Francis calls, his name appearing over Atlantic City.

I tell him I need to see him. He offers to pick me up but I tell him I want to walk.

"From the hospital?" he asks. "Are you sure?"

He's far away. Blocks uphill, my heels clicking the whole way.

———

His BEDROOM WALLS are white like a hotel room. His sheets are blue and grey, tucked neatly under the mattress. Sitting beside him, I shed all my weight against his shoulder. I drape my arms around his neck, my grasp tightening, clinging.

"I didn't know what to say. I never know what to say."

"She knows you care." He's talking about Jessa but I'm picturing the baby, swaddled in blankets and incubated warmth.

Trying, trying, trying.

"I meant it the other night," he says, his fingers flinching, tracing up my arm. "I'm scared for you sometimes."

I look at him.

"I didn't want you to walk all the way here," he says, "but I let you."

I lean in and kiss him. I try to fall back on the bed but he holds me up. He grips my thigh, his hands shaking, the tremors starting. I don't stop him. He slips his hand under the hem of my blue skirt. He gathers the fabric in his grasp, holding me by the waist as he pulls my tights, his touch caressing over my bare thighs, slipping between.

"Is this what you want?" he asks.

His breath caresses my neck, flushes my skin. I kiss him back, heat on my tongue, warmth filling my lungs. My grasp slips up his arms. My fingers cling tight against his muscles, his comfort. I pull at his shirt, showing him my need and my desire, things I've wanted all along.

Goosebumps flush my skin as he unbuttons my blouse. He slides the fabric down my shoulders. He unclasps my bra and he kisses my chest. His slow caress takes me. He lays me down on the bed, soft covers under my back, warmth circling me. He slips his fingers under my panties, eases his reach inside of me. The tremors fill me. My grasp slips over his shoulders. My fingers curl gently through his hair. He holds me close, pulls my legs around him.

I breathe in deep, taking in the scent of Atlantic City's boardwalk, the ocean in my lungs. I gasp and I moan. I ride the waves until I'm shaking.

———

MY PHONE VIBRATES on the nightstand.

There's a message from Jessa:

She made it through the night.

There's a new sight, my clothes on the floor, discarded. Francis lies beside me. His sheets are wrinkled but they're soft on my skin, his warmth reaching my side of the bed. I run a hand up his back. He stirs and opens his eyes. He touches my hand and I show him the message.

"I have to see her," I say.

He clings for a moment, but then releases his grasp. "Are you going to walk?" he asks.

I nod. I kiss him.

"Be careful," he says.

I step out of the bed and place bare feet on the floor. The wooden planks are laid out like a boardwalk, stretching outside, leading beyond.

IF SHE DIDN'T WANT THE ATTENTION, HER LIPS WOULDN'T BE SO RED.

GRIN ON THE ROCKS

She's a MILF who found me in the dark corner of a bar. She told me I was handsome and I flashed her my charmed smile, the one that usually buckled girls at the knees. Instead she slipped her hand around my arm. She pressed herself close, whispered seductively in my ear. She took me to her house. The next morning she rolled over and asked me if I wanted to rent it from her.

Now she's my landlord.

Now she's just another woman.

Now she's always at my door in her slutty shirts, telling me I owe her money.

"It's the tenth, Jonah." Today she's wearing sunglasses and my face is reflected in the wide lenses where her stare should be.

"I'm not stupid," I say, even though my gaze drops to her chest. Her black bikini shows through the white of her shirt. The deep neckline accentuates her cleavage. Perspiration beads along the tanned flesh of her breasts and slips into the valley between them.

You are stupid. You are.

"It's nearly the middle of the month," she says. "I have to pay for my kids' swimming lessons." She points toward her car where her two daughters sit in the back seat.

"I just started my new job," I say. "I don't even get paid until Friday."

She sighs and shakes her head, exaggerating. "So you're telling me I drove all the way down here for nothing?"

"Look," I say, reaching for my back pocket, fingers shaking around my wallet. I dig inside and hand her all the cash I have left. "There's two hundred here, two-fifty."

"That's it?"

"Swimming lessons can't cost any more than that."

Her jaw tightens, hard, rigid, sharpening her tiny frame. "I don't have the patience for this, Jonah. I really don't. I'm not running a charity." She puts her hand on her hip, drawing my gaze to the wooden beads dangling from the ties of her bikini bottoms. All I can remember is the way she rocked her pelvis while she was riding me, saying, *Oh God, Oh God, Oh God,* just like my mom used to when she couldn't handle being a single parent anymore.

"I'll get it," I say. "Like I said, I haven't even been paid yet."

"Next week," she says, pointing her finger against my chest. "You can bring it to me. It's too much of a hassle bringing the girls down here." The end of her fake French nail digs heat into me, right where my heart's throbbing.

"Fine," I say. "Whatever you want."

She nods, returns to her car. She tells her kids that she's in a hurry, that they're running late, that they're going to the pool now. She looks at me before she pulls out onto the street. My gaze slips to the newspaper on the doorstep. The front page features a photo of smiling young girls, bikini bodies burning on the beach, bold black headline announcing: *Summer's Here!*

I flip through the pages but there's never anything that interests me.

———

MOST OF WHAT MARK KNOWS about me are lies. He thinks that I like the outdoors, that I like the heat. He always works shirtless, mowing every lawn with his defenseless back braised red under the sun. The mole on his shoulder looks bigger, but he says he likes it when the girls stare.

"The cancer's getting you," I say, dragging a bag of grass clippings behind him.

He shrugs. "Cancer's gonna get everyone in this kind of heat."

"Have you even read about it?" I ask.

"About skin cancer?" He turns his head. "It's not even real cancer, man. They cut that shit right off. It's minor surgery."

"You can't always get rid of it all. It really depends on how deep the disease has gotten into your skin."

"Jesus, man," he says, smirking at he points at my sweat-stained shirt. "Go buy some fucking sunscreen if you're so fucking paranoid."

"I'm not paranoid," I say. "These are just facts."

He turns away, pushes the mower up the ramp and into the bed of his truck. "You sound like Cheryl," he says. "Melanoma's not so bad if you look at the entire spectrum of cancer." He twists the cap off his water bottle, chugs it back. "I mean, if I could pick a cancer, it'd be melanoma."

I stare at him, prying my sweaty gloves from my hands before clenching my fists tight.

He'd be better off with no cancer but he's already tangled up with his wife and his toddler son. Most nights he complains about Cheryl, about how she always has to have her way. Mark says he can never do anything right by her. When his phone rings and an argument arises, I imagine what Cheryl's voice sounds like on the other end, its piercing sound stabbing my insides, until Mark hangs up again. He's oblivious. He always laughs it off, makes the same joke about how he probably won't be getting laid for a while.

All it ever makes me think about is how much better things used to be, when men drank real drinks instead of the shitty weak beer that Mark digs out from the cooler in the back of his truck. He offers me one but I shake my head.

"It makes it easier, you know," he says. "Have a couple and you'll be drunk enough to finish the work without noticing the heat."

I take the beer. I crack open the tab and do what I do best, even though the cold barley taste of pale lager is never enough to calm the burn in my throat. It builds when I think too much. It's an ache I feel every time I take a breath.

Mark tilts his can back and takes a long swig of his beer. I remind him that there's still the back half of the complex to weed and he groans and wipes his brow.

"You feel like spotting me a couple hundred bucks?" I ask.

"What?" he asks.

"Speeding ticket," I say. "Yesterday afternoon."

He finishes the can and reaches for another. "What's wrong with you, man? This is the third one in two months."

I shrug and take another swig, pretending. "It's a curse."

He sets the beer down, reaches for his wallet. "I can't keep doing this, you know. Cheryl's going to find out."

"Stop being so honest," I say.

"You have to be honest when you're in my position." He flashes a look, acts like he's smarter even though he's the one guzzling the beer.

I tell Mark that I'll make it up to him, that I'll finish the work and he can enjoy his drink. That's what he does, enjoying his slow decay under the sweltering heat of the sun. He slugs the cans back with hard chugs just like my dad.

Even the low growl of the WeedWacker doesn't stop the memory of misery, the crack of the alcohol in his voice. He drank rum exclusively after the divorce, the scent of it hitting my face when he told me about my mom's postpartum depression.

"You know, your mom tried to drown you in the bathtub once," he said. "I saved you. I stopped her. I pulled you out. I fucking do her job while she's rotting? She couldn't even get out of bed back then and now all she does is thank Jesus for whatever it is she believes he did. She's like all of them, you know? They're all just greedy whores."

THIS HOUSE WITHOUT AIR-CONDITIONING is an oven in the heat wave. What little relief I feel quickly fades into the void between these four walls. I lay on the couch with the lights off, the windows shut and the curtains drawn. During the day I can't watch television. I can't use my computer. I can't cook, can't clean, can't use the dishwasher. The thermostat drifts a little higher whenever I try to get anything done.

At night it's easier to go out. It's easier to seek relief than to let the heat swell inside of me.

Usually it's a walk that ends up elsewhere: the pub, the club, spaces where I can feel less alone when surrounded by strangers.

I sit at the bar like men used to, facing the alcohol, all those cold glass bottles lined up on the wall. The bartender is the only person who ever stares back. The only thing he ever asks is if I want another drink, but sometimes he'll lean in with a warning, the sort that makes me wonder why the heat brought me here in the first place. He glances behind me and points to the girl smiling from across the room. She walks over and introduces herself, says her name is Bailey or Lindsay or Ashley.

Her name never matters.

Every girl comes wrapped in the same little dress, a flimsy tube of fabric that clings to her curves. Her hair's coiled up in hairspray, her presence covered in it, glitter and gloss and sexual aggression. She slips her hand over my arm and slithers her way in. I'd love for this to never happen, for me to be the gentleman instead of the idiot whose gaze always slips to her tits.

Little Sluts, my mother used to call them.

This one, she asks me what my name is.

"Matthew, Mark, Luke." I draw a breath and turn back to my drink. "What does it matter, really?"

"It'd be nice to know who I'm talking to." She stands there and I look at her again. I try to make eye contact because the last thing I want is to lose control. My heart throbs in my ears and my fingers cling too tightly to my glass.

"I'm not interested," I say. It's the easiest way to put it, the easiest way to spurn her advance without causing a scene.

"Asshole," she says, lips puckered aggressively around the last half of the word. They're glossy pink, like melting plastic. Her steps waver backward before she turns altogether, retreating back to her table of friends.

I return to my drink, the cold gin unable to tame the sound of her behind me, telling all of her girlfriends that I'm a real piece of shit.

Because you are, aren't you?

———

I WALK HOME, taking the pedestrian walk on the bridge. There's a girl coming from the opposite direction that makes me forget about the riverside breeze against my face. She's in regular clothes, in jean shorts and a shirt, but then I notice the shade of her lipstick and I can't help but clench my fists.

She notices. She makes eye contact and then she tenses. She keeps walking, her footsteps clicking on the sidewalk. She pulls her bag close to her chest.

I stare for too long. My jaw clenches and the girl looks away, breaks the connection as he passes.

Every flash of lipstick is a moving target, a trick. She's a lie, just like all of them. Her coiled locks slip over her shoulder. She walks faster, tightening her grasp into the strap of her purse. I bite my tongue; bite down while the words flood my skull.

One day you'll stop falling for it.

One day you'll spread her cancer.

One day you'll feel so much better.

If she didn't want the attention, her lips wouldn't be so red.

———

MY DAD used to take me grocery shopping before my mother had full custody. He'd buy discounted microwave meals and stack them on the conveyor. He'd gawk at the covers of the magazines in the checkout line.

"Looks kind of like your mother, doesn't she?" he asked, pointing at one of the covers.

The woman had my mother's dark hair and brown eyes, but her whitewashed skin looked ghostly against her bloodstained lips. He pulled the magazine from its metal slot and flipped through the pages to the full spread of the model that was supposed to be my mother, sprawled out half-dressed the way people never did in real life, her eyes lined in dark lashes like stingers that threatened to pierce my face if I leaned in too close.

My dad nodded and smiled. "Yeah," he said. "Just like her, right?"

———

MARK IS LIKE any other married man, slipping into a white plastic chair on the patio with a selection of empty cans beside him. Cheryl tries to rub his back while their son screams and pulls at her leg. She rolls her eyes and shakes her head, passing a glance at me before I get the chance to swallow the steeping flood she triggers in my chest.

I retreat to the inside, where most of Mark's birthday guests have retreated. The house's air-conditioned chill smells of fresh paint, of excess and excuses, a farce of a real relationship Mark seems to think he has. I only planned on staying a short while, and I'm the only one without a drink. Watching the girls makes my smile emerge. They're all strangers in the white light, outside of their comfort zone.

The trick is picking the right one.

She's the girl who stumbles into the crowded kitchen for a wine glass even though the bottle she's carrying is already half-empty. She sets it on the counter too hard. She digs through the cupboards, preoccupied, unaware of her place until I grab her attention.

"I don't know if you even need a glass at this point," I say.

"Probably not," she says, "but it helps to keep up appearances."

She chooses a glass and nearly knocks it over when she goes to pour the wine. I put my hand down over the base, holding it steady.

This close, the fake floral scent on her neck coaxes me to flinch when she offers me the glass. The red inside is deep and dark.

"Nobody needs to see how much I don't want to be here." I flatten my hand on the counter and meet her gaze.

"Am I being that obvious?" she asks.

"You're not being forced to stay here, are you?" Closing in, I reach for the charm of her necklace, this resin cube with a flower locked inside, delicate petals frozen in limbo. I take the plastic in my hand, holding her gaze until her cheeks darken to match her glass.

"You smell really good," she says.

My grip tightens around the charm. She glances away and takes another sip, the red dying her tongue as she stumbles over her words.

"You smell masculine, but like not like shitty cologne."

My fingers relax. I drop the necklace and watch her as she takes another drink. She smiles and then bites her lip over the expression. "I haven't spoken to anyone all night," she says. "Maybe you should just take me home."

The honesty soothes boiling pressure all the other women have ever left. I gather a breath of conditioned air and brace myself, gripping my fingers around her waist.

"Was that too obvious?" she asks.

"Maybe you should tell me what your name is," I say.

She lifts her hand and whispers in my ear like she's some kind of secret.

ELLEN AND I take a cab back to my place. The entire ride she's a giggling heap of drunken anticipation, her name a sticky mess of two syllables, lingering in the back of my skull. My tongue dries, sticks to the roof of mouth. I can't speak. I'm frantic, handing the driver my card, searching the depths of my pocket for my keys—sliding the right one into the lock. My breaths echo inside the heated darkness of the house when I pull her inside.

In the bedroom she clings to me, lets me pry her clothes off. She kisses aggressively, her mouth brimming with slurred words.

"God, I'm so drunk," she says, her desperation so hard her tits heave. "You can do whatever you want. Do whatever you want to me."

I kiss her back, but it's not long before she fades out, before her grasp slips from my shoulders and she passes out heaped on top of the sheets. I grab her frame and I shake her. A damsel moan slips from her mouth. Her head turns against the pillow. The overhead fan blows her dark curls over her pale face. She's a gone girl. She's sleeping beauty lost in consequence.

There are rules for this sort of scenario.

There are rules, but not everyone follows them.

I pull away from her, tendons flinching, making sweaty fists before I climb off the bed and draw a slow breath.

I throw the sheets over her naked flesh and spend another night sweating on the couch.

—

IN THE MORNING she gags in the bathroom. There's a chill in the house, a lowered sense of unease. I wait for her, staring at her purse on the coffee table. It's a small package of burden, glossy black patent leather that reflects my face when I lean forward.

She appears in the hall and I knock the purse over. It topples over the edge of the coffee table, falls somewhere on the other side. Her face is flushed, her cheeks red, hair greasy from the night. She's not the same girl. She leans against the wall and crosses her arms, her smile looking hesitant from behind her faded lipstick.

"What did I do last night?" she asks, her voice shaking.

She's a danger in this moment, seconds ticking away at the situation she's wound me into. She stands there reminiscent of other women, only she's asking me for answers instead of cornering me into her version of the truth.

"You passed out," I say. "I slept here. It seemed only decent."

She sighs, wipes her palm over her mouth. "I'm so sorry," she says. "I only really remember the cab ride. I remember walking through the front door."

You can do whatever you want.

I shrug. "It could have been worse."

She swallows, turns her gaze to the floor.

"You alright?" I ask.

"Yeah," she says. She wipes her lip and takes a seat beside me. "I've done this enough times to know that it's a shitty way to meet people."

"It's the easy way to meet people," I say. "Nobody ever said it was foolproof."

She laughs. "Well, you seem like a nice guy," she says.

I try to be a nice guy, yet my gaze proves otherwise, slipping over the scar on cleavage, just over her right breast. It's an old scar, long and faded into her skin.

"I've been with far more vile men than you," she says.

She catches me looking at the scar, but she's not like Jill. She turns her body away, makes herself a bigger secret, something to be unwound. The light reflects on her skin, makes it look creamy like overmilked coffee. She smiles, hesitant, her bare lips still glistening. She's smitten in the shadows, charmed by all the lies.

You're a nice guy. You're a nice guy.

I am. I offer her a ride home. She goes to look for her purse and I take her arm, suggesting that she probably left it at Mark and Cheryl's house. In the air-conditioned solace of my truck she tells me about her miserable job selling engagement rings at the jewelry store. She tells me how she ends every evening in the bathtub with a bottle of wine.

"The darker the better," she says.

She thanks me when I drop her off in front of her townhouse unit. I lean in, inhaling her scent—a wet garden, the scent of rain, something to tame this dry desert heat. Her skin makes me think of Mark's coffee—two creams, two sugar. He drinks it back every morning and always complains about being dehydrated every afternoon.

"I'd like too see you again," she says. "Is that okay?"

You shouldn't drink coffee.

"I'd like that," I say, and I smile because I'm a really nice guy.

———

MARK TUCKS a fresh cigarette behind his ear before hauling out the two red gas containers from the bed of his truck. They're older cans, plastic cans, bombs that could explode in the right circumstance. I'd tell him about all the articles I've read about smoking around gasoline, but he's never been the sort to heed warnings.

"Cheryl and Ellen used to work together a while back," he says, drawing the nozzle from the gas pump. He slips it into the opening of the first can. "Every party she'd have a bottle of Shiraz, wouldn't share it with anyone. Cheryl would always tell me stories about the dudes she was fucking."

"What does it even matter?" I ask.

He shrugs. "She's actually a blonde, you know?"

The way he says *you know* makes him sound like my drunk dad.

"Not sure why a blonde would ever want to ruin her hair like that," he says. "I've never seen the appeal of brunettes." He fills the container, transfers the nozzle to the second gas can. Then he looks at me. "How was she? Was she any good?"

My tongue's stuck, dry in my mouth, thinking of her, of the things I could have done.

"I don't share that kind of shit," I say, because gentlemen never tell.

"You probably should," he says. "You make it seem so fucking easy."

I look at him.

"All those bar stars," he says. "Your landlord."

"It's nothing," I say. "It's them. It's not me."

He sighs. "Cheryl was the only girl who ever threw herself at me, you know."

I bite my lip, watching him as he twists the cap back onto the gas can. He returns the nozzle back to its holder. Then he pulls the cigarette from behind his ear and retrieves his lighter from his back pocket.

"You're asking for it," I say.

"What?" he asks, lighting the end of the cigarette.

"You're going to die of cancer," I say.

———

ALL OF THE MOST-WATCHED VIDEOS have MILF in the title. It's the same word my friends used to describe my mom when she was bent over gardening in her denim shorts. Cut at mid-thigh, they weren't even attention-seeking. But all the women in the videos look like girls starved for attention, nothing like my mom, who didn't even flinch when my dad started getting drunk, started calling her a cunt all the time.

She said she was going to leave him: that she was going to take me away.

She divorced him and took me on a whale watching tour, said we were getting a fresh start. She kept commenting on how fresh the ocean was, but the ocean looked so angry, its edges sucking at the boat, lapping at it like a massive tongue. Its surface was like the back of a scaled demon roaring at me. Mom laughed beside me, thinking everything was supposed to be a lesson, saying, "You don't want to get thrown in there, Jonah. The ocean will eat you alive."

I take a sip of gin, feeling like the sissiest man God ever spoke to, and I shake my head, shake it all away because it's disgusting. The gin cools my mouth, vapour on my tongue, creeping down my throat.

On the screen there's a MILF that looks like Jill. She's tackled onto the floor, her dress pulled up. The guy spits in her face. He slaps her, calls her a whore. It's all good until the MILF starts to moan, her back curving with her lips. The ice in my drink is already gone. The heat's been affecting me my entire life. I'm sweating rivers, stroking myself until my dick gets sore. A groan comes up my throat and I throw the glass across the room, dousing the wall with the smell of gin and relief. All I want is to pour another drink but I just fucking can't with this kettle boiling in my lungs.

———

WHEN MARK GIVES me an envelope of cash on payday I take it directly to Jill. I pick through her mail-box. She subscribes to *Cosmopolitan*. The cover is a slew of bold capitalized words: *NAUGHTY, SAUCY, SEXY: 69 NEW WAYS TO GET ANY MAN*, all the self-help she needs. She's yelling at her kids, her voice sounding through the door. I knock and she answers with paint all over the front of her shirt. I hand her the mail, the envelope of rent money on top. She rifles through the bills, counts them out in front of me, shaking her head as her kids scream, complaining about how there isn't enough red paint, the colour on her shirt, and she winces like she's in pain.

"Not a good day?" I ask.

"No," she says. She smiles for a moment, but then her fingers twitch over the magazine. She stares down at the cover and sighs. The girls, they're making a mess of the papers and brushes while the red bleeds over the edge of the kitchen table.

"Sometimes don't you just want to kill them?" I ask.

She doesn't answer. It's awkward. It's fucking awkward, but I force myself to smile. Does she not remember, or is she just denying that she admitted it, that she hated being called Mommy.

"You know, my mom raised me by herself," I say. "She survived."

"Really?"

"I was probably worse than the two of them combined."

She looks down, her voice low. "It's hard. It's really fucking hard sometimes."

"I can imagine," I say, even though I can't. It just feels good to pretend, because all I can think of is that afternoon my mom was trying to refill the mower with a shitty plastic jerrycan, and I was whining, throwing a fit. She flinched, dropping the can, the plastic cracking. There was gas everywhere and she fell to her knees and started heaving, pleading, "Oh God, Oh God, Oh God, I can't do this anymore."

Jill finally smiles. "The kids go to their dad's on Friday," she says, taking a step forward, sliding her presence into my personal space. "It's a relief, getting a weekend to myself." She mimics the model on the magazine, every issue just a chest pressed forward, hip cocked, hand placed low, fingers pointing down like an arrow guiding me.

You're losing control.

"My mom never had any weekends to herself," I say. "She never had the chance to get away."

"Did you know your dad?" Jill asks.

I shrug, shifting my gaze, glancing down at the magazine. "He didn't really respect women."

She doesn't answer. She bites her lip and her pale face goes paler. She shifts, but she still holds her cover pose. My gaze drifts to the red on her torso. It fuels the heat in my chest. My shoulders tighten and I draw a breath. My tendons flinch. My fingers curl.

You're making fists.

"I hope your weekend goes well," I say before walking back to the truck.

On the way home I stop at the grocery store to buy a bag of ice for my drink, and I stand at the checkout counter, clutching the bag in both hands like it's a shield.

———

I PULL ELLEN'S PURSE out from under the coffee table. I pry it open and lay all of its contents on the table: her receipts, lotions, a manicure kit and her birth control. There's a charm on her keys, a capital letter "E" embedded with white rhinestones. Her lipstick's in the bottom corner of the bag. It's a shade called Berry Queen, bruised red, the slant on the stick curved to her lips. I draw the colour over my wrist, a line all the way down, back and forth, asking for attention. The lipstick goes on thick, greasy. The shade makes my lungs burn, makes my fingers start to shake.

I rub my fingers over the red and wipe it on my jeans, on the couch, the heat spreading.

The pressure builds inside my tightened fists. I unzip my pants and jerk off, picturing her leaning in front of the mirror, putting it on. I picture her kneeling between my knees, the greasy consistency of her mouth like hot oil burns on my dick.

You have to stop.

I keep stroking, thinking of her smile, of the void she had with her lipstick faded. My hard-on throbs in my grasp and I stroke until I'm exhausted and drenched in sweat, sitting on the couch useless and stupid and unable to get off.

I try to convince myself that this isn't cancer.

I wait until the perspiration cools my flesh and I draw a full breath of air, taking a sip of gin, its flavour diluted by the ice, chilling my throat all the way down.

Everything's going to be okay.

———

I BUY HER a hundred dollar bottle of wine using the money from her wallet. It's Shiraz in the most bruised shade of purple I could find. She pulls it from the gift bag at the end of our date, leaning awkwardly in the passenger seat of my truck.

"You didn't have to do this," she says.

"I wanted to." Easing in, I push her necklace aside and touch the scar on her chest. There's a silence in the haze. She stares at the wine, answers the question I can't ask.

"I used to mess around with this guy who was into knife play," she says.

For the first time of the night I actually meet her gaze, raising my eyes from the mottled flesh across her chest.

"He was more of a knife-enthusiast, I think. It was like he got off on just having one around."

"Was it bad?" I asked.

"I had to get stitches." She looks away, stares down at the bottle, at the darkness inside. "It was stupid, getting involved with him. I always kind of had a thing for fucked-up people. I don't know why." She shrugs her shoulders and then rubs her finger over the scar. "You do so much stupid shit when you're trying to figure yourself out."

"Do you regret it?"

"Usually I tell people that the scar's from a drunken accident." She clutches at the neck of the bottle, makes it seem like she's about to open it. "I tell them that I tripped and fell on my wine glass."

"That almost sounds more believable," I say.

She laughs with me. She laughs at herself. It's strange, because her honesty doesn't seem like some kind of *Cosmopolitian* trick to lure me in. Still, I follow her when she lets me into her house. She takes me to her bedroom and I have to fight the urge to punish her for it.

———

MARK REACHES into his cooler after work. Instead of beer it's cola. He says the caffeine is just as good, but I know exactly what was behind the change. He takes a swig and cringes, complains about the carbonation as he pushes the mower up the ramp and into the back of his truck.

His back is burnt.

The mole looks even bigger, looks about ready to swallow him whole.

———

THE NEXT TIME I see Jill is when she drops by my sweltering house in the early evening, asking me for rent before it's even due.

"I think you owe this to me," she says.

"Owe what?" I ask. "Tenants don't owe landlords favours."

She sighs and takes a step closer, presses her way into my space. "I think our situation is a little bit different than that, Jonah."

There's sweat on her chest, but this close I can smell the perfume she's sprayed there. It's vindictive, the tips she gets—the lessons she learns inside the glossy pages of her magazine. Her eyeliner must be waterproof, because even in this heat the black doesn't smear. She draws a breath that's slightly laboured. Her chest rises and I turn my head. I grip at the door frame, pressing down too hard, my blunt nails digging into the trim she'd never bothered to paint over, trim where she once traced the lines of her daughters growing up, growing taller, growing older, growing into women who will continue to manipulate men like me.

She puts her hand up, drapes her fingers over my shoulder.

"I'm seeing someone," I say.

"What?" she asks.

"Her name's Ellen."

She doesn't react, and that's when my fingers start shaking. The breath I draw shudders in my throat. I think of Ellen, of the position I've put myself in. I think of what little respect Jill has, digging her pastel pink nails into the fabric of my shirt, trying to steal me back, trying to make me property.

Little sluts.

Greedy whores.

All the things they say about women are true.

She meets my gaze, blinks her dark eyes, her lips making a subtle smirk. "Jonah, I just need you to be a friend to me right now. I've got two kids. I've got stuff to pay for."

"Then go and fuck somebody else," I say.

Her hand falls away. "Excuse me?"

I draw another breath, losing hold of my stance. My fingers grip at the door-frame, turning white against the trim.

"I'm your landlord, Jonah."

"No, you're not," I say. "You know exactly what you are."

Her lips purse, her eyes glistening for a split second, but then she blinks and replaces her look of fear with the dark-eyed glare of a woman sucking me inside of her.

"Do you want me to kick you out of here? Is that what you want?"

"What I want is some fucking air-conditioning," I say.

She leers, easing back a step, creating distance again. She sighs and crosses her arms. "Start paying your rent on time. Maybe I can help you."

Just like that, spit out, all chewed-up and red.

She turns walks back to her car. She starts the engine and glares as she drives away. Behind me all the heated air from the house tries to escape. Coiling my shaking fingers into my fist, I take a step outside, where it's colder, where there's some kind of relief.

———

MY FOOTSTEPS THROB all the way down 12th Street, the air thick in my lungs. The night fills in by the time I get to the park by the river. There's a woman in the arena parking lot, loading up her SUV, a fucking soccer mom in denim shorts and a pink shirt with a collar, her dark hair in curls. I watch her and feel the heat building. My strides widen, footsteps sounding heavy in the dead space of the empty parking lot. It's so late. There's nobody around. She turns just as I approach, but she's not fast enough to counter my tackle, not strong enough to push back when I shove her against the car.

I pull back a fist and it happens so fast, the hard sensation of my knuckles hitting her jaw.

She pushes at my face, her nails tearing my cheek. Her voice wails an animal moan, its pitch filling me with adrenaline. I punch her again and yank at her leash of tangled hair, covering her mouth, hauling her away from the car. Her feet drag gravel over all the white dividing lines of the parking lot. She stumbles when I get to the boat launch, and I pull her down the wooden boardwalk to the slough.

My feet sink into the sand. She loses her balance and I shove her down. I climb over her, press my knee into her chest. She tries to scream and I hit her harder, saying, "Shut the fuck up, shut your fucking bitch mouth."

The dark's festering: her face is a blur. Everything's a blur, but it doesn't matter who she is. All I want is to punish her, and I keep asking myself one question.

What's the worst thing you can do?

I ask her, "Are you scared, bitch? Are you fucking scared?"

She doesn't answer. Her moan deepens, and it gets stronger and more agonized the harder I hit.

A tingling sifts through my fingers with each strike. I punch at her chest, at her throat, her face, this jackhammer sensation making me curl my fingers, pull my arm back, bring my fist down again and again. The tingling stings with wet heat and I grip at her hair with my opposite hand, making tangles, tangles, everything tangled up because I can't even breathe anymore. There's only the world going black, and my voice is an ocean calling her a fucking cunt.

You fucking cunt, you greedy fucking useless cunt.

You, you, you.

This is you, isn't it?

You're pushing your elbow over this whore's throat and you're undoing your pants because you know it's the worst possible thing you can do. Her throat pulses against your hand. Her heart's beating and it's shaped like fear. Your dick isn't even hard and you tell her, "Suck me off and it'll be over faster."

She only moans. You climb up and shove your dick in her mouth. She tries to suck it, but her mouth feels like nothing. You can't even recognize her face because it's filled with red. She's a plastic gas can leaking fuel, weak and flimsy, and you hold her down while you stroke yourself, get yourself hard, because sex wasn't what you were thinking about, but this is just the worst thing you can possibly do to her.

You rip her shorts: tear them down. She's not even struggling when you spread her legs. It's so easy and she just takes it when you spit on her cunt and shove yourself in. You choke her, pushing your weight onto your hand. You're staring her down and she knows her place and you're telling her, "That's it, bitch, that's it, that's fucking it."

You hit her again and again, each strike followed by her guttural moan. You take her, pull her hair, drag her toward the river and push her face into it, washing yourself, washing the evidence away. The water's so cold and dark that it'll eat her alive and that's the worst thing, the worst possible thing, because she didn't even have the chance to prove otherwise.

You leave her there. You walk away. And for the first time you feel a breeze blowing, cooling the sweat on your face. You exhale and it tastes like gin, its strength chilled over rocks. You walk home and the pavement feels like ice under your feet. It feels like coming, because you haven't been able to for weeks and that's what relief feels like.

———

I'M IN THE BATHROOM, putting gel in my hair and combing it back like I did that night at the bar. My phone rings. It's Mark. "I know it's your day off," he says, "but I picked up a job near the airport and I know you need the money."

He offers to pay for lunch at the airport, and I meet him there with scratches on my face and scabs on my knuckles.

"What happened to you, man?" Mark asks.

"Bitches be crazy," I say, because he seems like the type and he laughs.

"Your fists, too?" he asks.

"It was a rough night at the bar," I say.

"Oh yeah?" he asks.

"Yeah," I say, and that's the end of it.

He reaches behind him, tries to scratch at the peeling burns on his back.

On the table there's a copy of the newspaper, an article on the front page in bold black: *Woman assaulted, raped at McArthur Park*.

It tells me everything I can hardly remember: the woman, the victim, how she was found unconscious, barely breathing, how she's currently recovering from multiple injuries: heavy bruising, a split lip, broken teeth, a broken rib, a fractured jaw.

All of it's a blackout in my head, and all I remember is approaching her from behind, her dark hair and her Jeep Cherokee, the same car my mom used to drive. The article uses the term "anger rapist" because that's apparently what I am. It says I might strike again. The warning words speak in my head like a voice, like how the Bible used to speak to my mom, saying, "You're pervasively angry" and "You're aggressive and violent," and "You are Jekyll and You are Hyde."

There's a picture, a composite sketch, clear lines defining sunken jaws and dark eyes, my hair greasy, uneven. I lick my lips. A drop of sweat beads on my forehead and I'm wondering, "Is that what you look like?"

The article says that every woman should be aware of you, this pencil sketch of you, one woman's memory of her night with you.

"You okay?" Mark asks, still scratching, still unable to do anything about his position in life.

I look up and fold the paper, covering the article. The air conditioning kicks in above us, its white noise cooling the sweat. "I'm great," I say, and a smile forms on my face that takes no effort to make.

"DO YOU WANNA KNOW HOW DISGUSTING I AM?"

MASTURBATING MEGAN'S
STRIP MALL EXHIBITION

A group of fresh-faced boys walked into the store, their cocky laughter filtering through the city's largest selection of adult movies, toys and novelties.

Strip Mall: Strip down to your naughty side!

I pressed my pelvis against the stool behind the till. Leaning over the counter, I asked to see their ID's. Each one of them handed me their cards, their eighteen-year-old fingers shaking and sweaty.

"Is this your first time here?" I asked.

They nodded, shoulders tight, voices muted, the expanse of Strip Mall before them. The boys spread out and wandered solo between the aisles. I focused on one kid with a shaggy haircut and dark-washed jeans. He ran his hand along the shelves, fingers just inches away from the movies.

The clock ticked above me, the only sound in the store that made my heart throb against my chest. I lifted my skirt and pressed my bare crotch against the stool. Its cold metal surface forced me to draw a breath.

The shaggy-haired kid picked up a DVD, his smile widening, the awkwardness spreading. "You guys wanna rent *My Ass Is Haunted*?"

The boys grouped together again. Their laughter overpowered the sound of the clock, ruining the moment. I pushed my skirt down. My fingers clenched over the hem, nails scratching against my bare thighs.

The clock kept ticking, an endless lack of relief.

———

THE BOYS TOOK FOREVER, taking turns hitting each other with the whips and paddles from the bondage bargain bin. I sat on the stool, my gaze on the door, fingers rapping against the counter, restless sweat breaking out on my forehead.

I heaved a sigh when Steve arrived. The boys looked up, their gazes glued to his small stature as he walked toward the BBW section at the back of the store.

The boys exchanged glances with each other, snickering at Steve, laughing when he picked up *Horny Holly Hanson's Hungry Hungry Humps*. Steve turned his head, looking the shaggy-haired boy in the eye. "Something wrong?" he asked.

The boys shook their heads. They put the whips back into the bin and then mumbled to each other before leaving the store.

Steve smiled as he walked up to the till. "Rite of passage shoppers?"

"You couldn't have waited longer to show up?" I asked, looking down at the movie. On the cover was a curvy woman on all fours, her ass arched up like a cat. I rang it through as the boys' laughter echoed outside.

"I didn't mean to ruin your fun," Steve said.

"They weren't cutting it," I said, putting the DVD into a plastic Strip Mall bag. "I didn't want them to be here when Nelson showed up."

He shook his head. "I should be offended that I'm not your favourite customer."

I looked up.

"I'm the only customer you actually talk to," he said.

"You *are* my favourite customer," I assured him.

He laughed just as hard as the boys. "Don't shit yourself, Megs. I know I'm not your type."

———

THE SECOND HAND TICKED over the store, timing his footsteps. It was quarter after eleven. I pressed my thighs together, building the tension, the pressure. Nelson walked in and the burning erupted between my legs. I reached under my skirt and buried my fingers in the wetness.

Nelson's name wasn't really Nelson, but he looked like a Nelson, a somber, middle-aged man who tucked his button-front work shirts into his jeans, a man with a wedding ring and faded family pictures in his wallet. He walked slowly through the aisles, taking his time, never looking up from the shelves.

The clock ticked harder, timing a careful pace toward the hardcore masturbation videos. His shoulders rose and fell, and I rubbed my clit to his awkward selection of a movie. I pushed my skirt back down when he turned and approached the till.

He placed *Scrumptious Stuffed Sluts: Volume 1* on the counter. On the cover was a collage of girls taking on zucchinis and rolling pins and full cuts of salami. He pulled cash out of his wallet, his fingers flinching over the bills.

"How are you doing tonight?" I asked.

"I'm fine." He put a twenty down on the counter.

I took the bill and gave him his change, my wet fingers brushing over his palm, as the clock's ticking throbbed between my legs. My toes clenched in my shoes. I rang the movie through and reached for a plastic bag.

"I have my own," he said, showing me the reusable grocery bag in his hand. He snatched the movie from the counter and slipped the it inside.

I tore the receipt from the till but he held up his hand.

"Have a good night," I said.

"You, too!" He wrapped the bag over the DVD and went for the door.

I lifted a slat over the blinds covering the front window, and watched him unlock his car. He threw the bag into the passenger seat. My hand drifted under the hem of my skirt, my fingers slipping between my lips, over my clit.

I came to the sound of him driving away.

I CHECKED THE IDs of a group of girls who went straight for the wall of dildos and vibrators. They were pretty girls, like the ones in high school, and they ignored me just like the girls in high school did. They never asked me questions, so I made a fist and spoke up like Steve.

"Seriously, if you guys really want to get off, you need the Magic Wand."

One of them laughed. The rest of them turned away, the clock ticking like it used to in every high school classroom, backing all the whispers, the snickers, the hesitant laughs. My throat tightened, but the laughter continued as the girls went through the store. One of them turned back to look at me, her pink lips twisted into a sneer, making me feel like Masturbating Megan all over again.

In high school, the girls used to huddle close, their voices pitched and pierced, saying, *"She's the girl who masturbates in class."*

High school was where the clock started ticking, me with no friends, sitting in the back of every room. Somehow it always felt better, hearing the second hand time the awkward silence that followed whenever the teacher asked one of the boys a question. It made me so wet, watching them flinch, listening to their voices stutter. I'd feel the gears of the clock shifting in my cunt and I'd spread my legs under the desk. I'd have to deal with the pressure.

It didn't take long before somebody noticed.

"Oh my God," one of the girls said. She pointed at one of the dildos on the wall, the big purple one the shape of a fist. "That's so gross. Who would ever want to shove that up their vajayjay?"

"For fuck's sake, just call it a goddamn vagina," I say.

The girls look up and stare.

"Just call it what it is," I say.

I TOOK HOME EVERY MOVIE that Nelson rented. The first scene in *Scrumptious Stuffed Sluts: Volume 1* was of a blonde straddling the tapered end of a butternut squash. I pictured Nelson in his basement, the lights out, and the TV volume low. I pictured him dick in hand, his fist clenched, thick with lube while he jerked himself to a finish. I thought about how restrained his groan sounded when he came. I rubbed my clit to the idea of him staining the couch, his relief only temporary, his breath getting frantic when his wife's footsteps sounded upstairs. I pictured him rushing to eject the DVD from the player, having to hide the case, the evidence, and the shame.

I never felt so close to him, climaxing with the blonde on the screen. Hot squirt gushed across my coffee table, all over the DVD case. I thought about the jizz-stained fingerprints he'd covered it with and I said his name aloud, my gasps matching the frantic ticks from the collection of vintage anniversary clocks on my bookshelf.

"Nelson, Nelson, Nelson, Nelson, Nelson."

———

STEVE DRUMMED HIS FINGERS against the counter to the pace of the second hand. It was half past eleven. Nelson hadn't stopped by in over a week.

"Stop it." I put my hand over Steve's. His skin was lukewarm.

"The Internet was made for girls like you," he said. "You could post an ad, post a video. You'd get exactly what you want."

"And what's that?" I asked.

"Companionship."

I looked down at the counter.

"You know what'll happen, right?" Steve glanced down at the cover of *Scrumptious Stuffed Sluts*. His brows furrowed. "Eventually he'll cave. Eventually he'll get tired of energy drink cans and zucchinis."

"You keep coming here," I said.

"Because I know what I like," he said. "I keep things simple. He only started simple, and soon enough this store won't be able to offer what he's going to need. Soon enough he'll be jerking it in front of his computer to a Japanese chick shoving cockroaches up her snatch."

The clock wouldn't stop ticking.

"He's an addict, Megs. There's nothing you can do."

I didn't believe him. I didn't want to. After work, I stopped by the grocery store and bought a bottle of lube and a cut of salami.

———

NELSON CAME IN the next night, looking rushed, frantic. He didn't take nearly as long as usual to pick out *Great American Challenges*. The cover had a picture of a girl taking on a purple fist dildo like the one on the wall. He brought the movie back the following night.

"Was it not good?" I asked.

He shrugged. His gaze dropped and he looked out at the expanse of the store before turning back to me. "It wasn't my thing."

"What is your thing?"

"I just, I'm not really..."

The ticking clock made him sound like all the cocky boys in high school. I pressed myself against the edge of the stool, ground my pelvis against the seat. I leaned over the counter but he didn't look up, didn't look at me.

"You like insertions, right?"

He braced his hand against the counter and nodded. "Yeah," he said. His fingers curled into a fist. "I'm uh, well... I'm into that."

"I can probably order in something for you," I said.

He met my gaze. His posture stiffened. His gaze dropped back to the cover of the DVD case, his lip curling at the plastic toys, fake dicks, simulated pleasure.

"I'll dig around. I'll find something. You want, like, live stuff, right? No animation?"

He nodded, the slow bob of his chin matching the ticking of the clock. My pussy dripped against the edge of the stool. I shuddered, but he didn't ask me if I was okay. His fist started shaking over the counter. He swallowed and pulled away.

"It shouldn't be too long," I promised.

———

A WOMAN WALKED IN as I was ringing through Steve's favourite movie, *Big Bodacious Babes in Brazil*. The woman looked at Steve and then at the movie on the counter, her lips turning a sneer. She had a worn out face and circles under her eyes. She walked toward the till clutching a reusable grocery bag.

"Can I help you?" I asked.

She turned the bag over on the counter and shook out all eight volumes of *Scrumptious Stuffed Sluts*.

I felt Steve's gaze, but I stared at the woman, at her uneven skintone. All I could think about was how much better she'd look if she'd put on makeup.

"I found these in his filing cabinet," she said. "He told me everything. I *made* him tell me everything."

I stared too long. Her eyes narrowed and I shook my head.

"My husband," she hissed. "You know who he is. He's in here all the time."

"That's none of my business," I said. "I just work here."

"You're supporting this," she said. "You're ruining families, ruining lives. You have no idea how long this has gone on." Her chest heaved. She blinked and her eyes got red, wet. "I cancelled the Internet. I spent nights talking with him. He promised he was over it and now he's just getting all his filth from here."

The clock ticked. I looked down at the movies, the girls on the covers even filthier than me, taking on wine bottles and cucumbers and pillar candles.

"We have *kids*," she said.

My lips smirked. "Like I told you, I just work here."

She blinked and the tears slipped down her cheek. She took a breath and looked me over, judging my low-cut shirt, my short skirt, and the streak of pink in my hair. She stared too long, just like all of the girls in high school used to.

"It's disgusting what you do," she said.

"You shouldn't involve yourself in this," Steve said.

"I'm trying to keep the store in business."

Steve walked around the counter. He crossed his arms. "He's not a sex-addict, Megs. He gets off to girls on a screen."

My heart pounded in my ears. Heat rushed up my chest. I blinked and felt the burning behind my eyes. "I don't care about his marriage."

"He doesn't want anything to do with you," Steve said.

I set my camera up in front of my bookshelf, the clocks ticking behind me. I took the salami out of the fridge, getting wet thinking of Nelson seeing me, seeing Masturbating Megan for the first time.

"You're fucking hungry, aren't you?" I asked.

His eyes were the lens, watching me lube up the meat, watching me spread my legs. The meat was cold, sliding in, stretching me out. The clocks ticked. My breaths got heavier, laboured.

"Do you wanna know how disgusting I am?"

The salami warmed inside of me. I opened myself, pushed it in deeper. The clocks ticked and my heart pounded, head spinning so fast I felt like exploding.

There was an envelope in the return bin. Inside were the broken disc pieces of *Masturbating Megan Munches Massive Meat: Volume 1.* Inside were family photo of Nelson and his wife at a park. They were sitting on a playground bench with his two little daughters. On the back of the photo was a note his wife had written with a black Sharpie:

YOU'VE BEEN CAUGHT, SLUT! STAY AWAY FROM MY HUSBAND!

I flipped the photo over again. Nelson's wife was wearing make-up in the photo. Her hair was shiny and straight, her pink lips turned, smirking.

Steve would have lectured me, but Steve didn't have the ability to understand.

The sound of the clock was overtaken by the sound of a car pulling into the parking lot outside. I peeked through the blinds. The car was Nelson's. His shadow was slouched inside, his head against the dash, hands gripping the wheel.

I didn't have to stay away from him. He would always come back. He knew me better than anyone.

It was impossible to feel guilt, impossible to feel anything but the heat dripping down my leg.

The second hand on the clock went tick, tick, tick.

THAT'S JUST THE WAY MY DREAMS ARE. THEY'VE BEEN NIGHTMARES SINCE I STARTED UNIVERSITY.

COLLEGE GLACIERS

The cab driver is the kind of guy I'd fuck in my dreams. He's got dark hair and olive skin and thick bench-pressed triceps. He's probably got a monster dick, a big dick that's actually a monster, a throbbing snake with a face. That's just the way my dreams are. They've been nightmares since I started university.

I pop another pill.

"Can you drive a little faster?" I ask. "I really need to get to my dorm."

"Relax," he says. "It ain't that late, Cherry."

"Cherry?"

"Cherry," he says. "Like the fruit."

"I know what cherries are."

"Well, that's sweet," he says.

I sit back and run my tongue over my teeth, picturing cherries, red stains of failure. Anxiety fills my chest. I swallow and grind my teeth. The sound vibrates through my ears. It's how a glacier must sound when it moves and scrapes the earth. It's called "glacial abrasion" and it's going to be on the exam tomorrow. The professor said so.

"I really need to get to my dorm," I say again.

"Of course you do," he says. "Girls like you always gotta be somewhere."

The streets look like they're covered in a miserable haze through the cab's tinted windows. Downtown's like a big garden full of ghosts, bright girls stumbling through the streets in their glitter dresses. Bass filters from the nightclubs. The sound throbs in my skull, makes my heart beat erratically.

I try to swallow but my mouth's already too dry.

"You don't look okay, Cherry," he says. His brows furrow, and I meet his gaze through the rear-view mirror. His eyes are dark, little demons staring at me instead of the road.

"I need to study," I say.

"In that dress?" he asks.

My fingers flinch, pulling at the fabric. The dress is white with printed cherries. The fabric is tight around my thighs. Ashley gawked at me when I first tried it on. She said I looked so skinny. She said she was so jealous she couldn't even stand it. She didn't even care that I was failing Geography.

"In that dress, you look like you belong downtown," he says.

"It's not my dress," I say.

"Doesn't change the fact that you're wearing it," he says.

"My friend wanted me to wear it," I say. My fingers clench and I tug at my seat belt, the pills kicking in like coffee jitters, just all kinds of worse.

"You must have ditched her tonight," the driver says. He approaches the rest light at the intersection and I feel his reflected mirror gaze, snake eyes staring.

"She's not really a friend," I say. "I don't hang out with her much."

"No?" he asks.

"We don't have that much in common."

The light changes and he puts his foot back on the gas.

I look outside again. Two girls are yelling at each other on the sidewalk, fully made up with spray tans and clip-in extensions. I imagine their purses crammed full of credit cards, condoms and lip gloss, concealed within glossy cheetah prints with glitzy metal brand names.

My purse is velvet vintage.

My purse doesn't even contain makeup, just my cash and my ID and a bag full of pills.

I pop another one and catch the driver looking at me. He pulls off Main and drives past the coffee shops and the pharmacy, then turns onto Columbia and cruises past the hospital. The lit windows beam bright in the night.

"Do you think she's mad?" he asks.

I look up.

"Your friend," he says. "She's probably pissed at you."

"I never go out," I say. "She knows that I've got an exam tomorrow. She knows I can't fail Geography."

"What happens if you fail?" he asks.

"I can't," I say. "I'm not going to fail. That's why you have to get me back to my dorm."

"Are you no good at Geography?" he asks.

The layered effect of the pills burns at my insides. My chest rattles. My fingers clench. The passing sights blur in the dark. I shut my eyes. Behind them is just a rush of black shadows, ghosts in my head, pieces of myself melting away with the receding glacier that's going to be on the exam. The professor said so.

"I asked you a question," the driver says.

"What?" My heart's throbbing and I glance at him in the rear-view mirror.

"Are you no good at Geography?" he asks again. "Do you not know how the world works?"

He drives further and my fingers start shaking. I glance at the read-out on the meter beside the steering wheel, the red numbers flickering. I can't focus on them. I reach into my purse for another pill.

"You look scared, Cherry," he says.

"Stop calling me Cherry."

"I just call it as I see it." He looks me over as he drives over the set of speed bumps at the campus entrance. The car shakes and the pill slips out of my grasp and under his seat. "You don't know anything," he says.

My heart's pounding, making an ache out of my chest. He approaches the dorms at the slow parking lot speed limit and my heart echoes uneasy in my ears. I squint to read the display beside the steering wheel. I peel out the only bill from my purse and hand it to him. He takes the money and shrugs.

"Take care of yourself, Cherry."

I pull at the door handle, anxiety-ridden, scrambling to pull the strap of my purse over my shoulder, but it catches the door and falls onto the pavement. My pills spill out, along with my photo ID. The picture on the card is shitty. My face looks hollow and my eyes look too wide. I scramble for the card, but then he gets out of the car and pushes me aside to pick up the bag of blue pills.

"No, please," I say. "I need those. I really do."

He smiles and holds up the bag. "They're not in a bottle," he says. "You typically get Adderall in a bottle, don't you?"

"I need those to study. You don't know what it's like."

"I know plenty," he says. "You college girls all want the same thing."

"You're just going to sell them to somebody else," I say, reaching for the bag.

"Look, Cherry," he says, stepping back. "You come to the gym one day, I'll get you determined, but this shit, it makes your brain all red."

He stares too long, takes a step too close.

"You've all got sad eyes," he says. "Sad kitten eyes."

He gives the pills back to me, pushes the bag against my torso and waits until I grasp it before he backs away. "The gym I work at," he says. "It's downtown, under the Grotto Bar. It's in a basement but it ain't so bad." He backs away, climbs into the cab and drives off.

The pills shuffle in the plastic like plucked bits of myself. The jitters taper and I start to shake for real, because every time the pills recede I'm left with a new landscape. There's outwash plains and terminal moraines and drumlins.

I swallow.

It's all going to be on the exam tomorrow. The professor said so.

HE COUGHED UP PHLEGM AND
FELT IN HIS POCKET, HIS
FINGERS TIGHTENING, CURLING
INTO HIS PALM, MAKING FISTS.
THERE WAS NOTHING THERE,
JUST THE KEYS TO HIS CAR,
HIS HOUSE—HIS HOME.

SLIPPERY SLOPES

The kid on the white bike was a nuisance, lurking in the shadows of the Pineview Estates parking lot with his flashlight and his uncoiled wire coat-hanger, leaving marks on the cars, scratches on paint, on windows. He'd steal things. Never important things, but they were things nonetheless. Having just chased the kid out of the parking lot, Luke Truman dug through his pocket for his brand new pack of cigarettes.

The cigarettes were purchased in a lapse of judgement, but Luke unwrapped the package, wondering what he would have done if he hadn't tripped and lost his grasp of the kid's baggy sweatshirt. He wiped his forehead and brought a fresh cigarette to his lips. Frayed nerves twitched through his fingers as he ignited his lighter. He inhaled the smoke, the nicotine bringing on a foreign sense of relief that he vaguely remembered.

Four years, it had been.

He probably should have told Anita he'd been having cravings, but he hated the idea of worrying her. She already knew that he wasn't sleeping through the night. Luke blamed his anxiety on work, but even after putting in a good day at the pulp mill he'd still wake up in a pool of his own sweat. He tried opening the bedroom window, tried sleeping on top of the sheets, but he could never get a full night of rest when his body was so taut with nervous ticks.

He started taking walks through the neighbourhood, the night air cooling his flesh and doing little else. One night he ended up at the 7-11. There was a guy with a backwards cap leaning against the side of the building, inhaling a cigarette, the smoke floating upward. Luke had craved relaxation for so long, so he walked into the 7-11 and pulled out his wallet.

The smokes sat unopened in Luke's pocket for a week, but their burden now felt a little bit lighter with a lit cigarette between his fingers. The smoke tickled his lungs when he breathed in. He coughed and hacked up phlegm, its thickness sliding up his throat. He spat on the cement, his fingers flinching, shaking.

Luke stared out at the cars in the complex parking lot, safe for the night because of his action. He finished the cigarette and dropped it, scraping it against the cement with the sole of his shoe. It was just one cigarette, but the pack lingered in the chest pocket of his jacket, his heart beating against it.

He slept on the couch so Anita wouldn't smell the smoke.

———

He was up before Anita, printing out notices to pass to the neighbours. He didn't hear her footsteps when she walked downstairs. She took one of the notices from the printer:

The little shit on the white bike is back and looking into your cars and trucks. Be vigilant! Lock up and keep valuables away and out of sight. I chased him out of here at 1 AM and almost caught him. Lucky for the both of us!!!

"Three exclamation points?" she asked.

"Does it make me sound stupid?"

"You shouldn't have chased him," she said.

Luke took the notice from his wife's grasp. "He would have stolen something."

"It was just CDs," she said.

"They were the boys' CDs."

"You hated those things. You regretted buying them the second you played them in the car."

Luke remembered them, the songs about banana phones, baby belugas, robins in the rain. What was worse was seeing his twin sons upset over the loss—Andrew and Oliver, identical as the sound of their cries.

"This isn't about the CDs," Luke said. "It's about some shit kid taking what isn't his."

Anita put her hand on his shoulder. "I just don't want to see you get all wound up about this," she said. "You're stressed enough as it is."

Luke hesitated. He sighed and looked up at his wife. "I'm just doing what I can, Ani."

She took his hand and placed it over her belly, where their third child was kicking. "Since four AM," she said. "He knows when you're upset."

"He?"

Anita smiled. "He sure moves around like the boys did. He kicks enough for the both of them."

"You want another boy?" he asked.

She smiled and leaned in. Luke could smell her coconut milk lotion. He felt her soft lips against his furrowed brow and held his breath until his lungs ached.

"He's going to be a handful," she mocked.

Luke exhaled slowly, pulled his hand from his wife's stomach, and turned to the stack of notices from the printer.

———

LUKE TOOK THE BOYS to the park on Sunday afternoon so Anita could cook dinner. He thought that he might have a chance to sneak away and smoke a second cigarette while the boys played, but his retired neighbour Joe was already at the park flying his remote control helicopter. The boys let go of his hands so they could play on the monkey bars, and Luke slipped his hand into his pocket, fingers flinching around his lighter.

"Sounds like you had an interesting night last night," Joe said.

"You could say that," Luke said. "He was going to break into your car."

"Really?" Joe asked. "He wouldn't have found much, the lousy punk. I never understood kids like that, ruining a decent neighbourhood with their juvenile shit."

"He'll be back," Luke said.

"Is Anita worried?"

"She's more worried about me than she is about anything else," he said.

Joe laughed, his gaze on the helicopter in the sky. "Nothing worse than when your wife starts to worry about you."

Luke let go of the lighter. He watched the helicopter float through the sky, rubbing at the stubble on his neck.

"Wouldn't it be scary if she was having twins again?" Joe asked.

"She's not having twins," Luke said, gritting his teeth. "The technician said so."

"Technicians make mistakes sometimes."

"I saw the twins. I know what twins look like." Luke's fingers tightened. His jaw shifted.

"I'm just messing with you, Luke. You're going to be fine."

Joe let go of the control and slapped Luke's shoulder. The helicopter twitched in the sky.

———

THE DAY AFTER he handed out the notices, Luke arrived home from work and noticed that the neighbour had left his truck unlocked. He unloaded the groceries from the car and peered through the truck's window. An open wallet was left in the driver's seat. Luke shook his head, staring at the neighbour's driver's license photo, twenty-six and fresh-faced, spending evenings out smoking on the patio. It was what Luke used to do in that fifteen minutes after he got home from work, was indulge in relief.

He went inside and brought the groceries upstairs. Anita dug through the bags. "Did you not get any bread?" she asked.

"Dammit," Luke said. He scratched at his forehead and sighed.

"We really need bread," she said.

"Can't the boys have something other than sandwiches for lunch?"

"I already promised them sandwiches. You know how they get."

"Alright," he said, and he pulled out his keys again.

He passed the neighbours truck and he stared at the open wallet on the seat. All he could taste was tobacco when he breathed in. He opened the driver's door of the truck and pushed the lock down. He slammed the door harder than he should have. Luke stared at the neighbour's youthful face and gritted his teeth. He couldn't remember ever forgetting his wallet anywhere. He couldn't remember ever forgetting to lock his car door.

———

THE PACKAGE OF CIGARETTES lingered in his pocket all day. The cigarettes shifted every time he took a step. Luke thought about the trial he'd put himself through when he'd quit the first time, how terrible it was with two newborns crying all night long. It was bad, but then it got better. He and Anita used to stay up late together, rocking their sons back to sleep. Anita gave Luke his free time. He started jogging. He got in shape. His cough went away.

Now Luke stood in the rain on his lunch break. He thought about buying the bread the day before, standing in the line-up at the grocery store, his grasp tightening around the loaf. He thought about Andrew and Oliver eating their warped bologna sandwiches. He pulled out the cigarettes, counted the two he'd smoked since he'd first bought the package.

He knew it was desperation, that two smoked cigarettes didn't mean he'd relapsed. It was all just a lapse in judgement, and it wasn't worth having to go through the process of quitting again, not with another baby coming. Anita worked at the same daycare the boys went to, but she would soon be on maternity leave and Luke would have to support them all. He thought about the bills, about the comments Anita sometimes made about someday getting a bigger car, a bigger house, a real house with four bedrooms and a big backyard.

His heart started to pound. He went to put the cigarettes back in his pocket but his fingers flinched over the cardboard package. His boss, Walter, approached. He nodded at the box.

"I didn't know you smoked, Luke," he said.

"Not really," Luke said, shrugging. "I'm just in the process of quitting."

"Well, you can't be doing too well if that's a new pack," Walter said.

"Yeah, I know," Luke said. His throat tightened and he pulled out a fresh cigarette, needing something to hold onto. He tried to hold it steady between his fingers.

"Mind if I bum one?" Walter asked. "I'll be doing you a favour."

"No," Luke said, and he held out the pack.

Walter took one, pulled out his lighter. "I've tried to quit four times, you know? I tried everything. One time my wife dragged me to a hypnosis seminar that promised results. Obviously it was just a crock of shit." Walter lit the end and took a puff. "It's all just one slippery slope."

He passed Luke the lighter. Luke took it and hesitated. Standing in the cold, in the rain, his body wracked with shivers, he tried to remember what relief once felt like.

"You okay?" Walter asked.

Accidents happened. They happened all the time. He thought about the night Anita told him about the baby. He couldn't hold back the dread and she noticed. She reached for him. She held his face in her hands. She said that life was full of the unexpected, that they were going to make their situation work for them.

"Luke, you okay?" Walter asked.

"I'm fine," Luke said. He brought a cigarette to his lips.

"Most ex-smokers say that quitting was the hardest thing they've ever done," Walter said.

"Yeah?" Luke asked, his finger flinching over the wheel of the lighter.

"Must be nice to actually kick the habit, to never have to buy another pack."

Luke stared ahead at the dark smog of pulp mill emissions, thick smog that sailed up and canvassed the overcast sky. His grip tightened around the lighter. He brought it up and lit the end of his cigarette, the nicotine heat seeping deep down into his lungs as he inhaled. He fought hard not to cough in front of Walter, but he did anyway.

———

HE SLIPPED INTO a new routine. He smoked on his lunch breaks. He smoked in the car on the way home from work, the window rolled down. He smoked when he couldn't sleep at night, walking circles around the parking lot. He searched the shadows for the kid on the white bike. He smoked the whole package by the end of the week.

He took the boys to the park on Sunday. They wanted helicopter rides. They pulled him into the field and jumped and pleaded.

Andrew said, "Daddy, spin us!"

Oliver said, "Both of us!"

When the boys were younger he used to act as a centrifugal force, swinging them one at the time, their trusting grasps clinging tight. He kept them rotating the right distance, kept them from spinning off-kilter. He used to close his eyes and feel the calm of the centre, the air brushing his face, whispering in his ears.

He spun Andrew first, but the black darkened behind his eyes. He held his breath and grew dizzy. His lungs tightened. His throat burned. His head throbbed.

He slowed to nothing and Andrew skidded back on the grass and laughed. Oliver pulled at Luke's shirt, begging for a turn. Luke gasped and fell to his knees and coughed. The boys screamed, their kid shrieks filling his ears.

"Daddy, Daddy, Daddy!"

He said, "You guys are too big for this."

He gasped for breaths. He wanted a smoke.

He coughed up phlegm and felt in his pocket, his fingers tightening, curling into his palm, making fists. There was nothing there, just the keys to his car, his house—his home.

———

HE WOKE to the sound of Anita's voice over him, her hand on his chest, his sweat soaking though the sheets again.

"Luke, you're practically lying in a puddle."

He sat up, the air against his bare chest. "I'm sorry," he said. He wiped his forehead and climbed out of the covers.

"Open the window," she said.

"I'll just go for a walk," he said.

She reached out. "Come back to bed," she said. "We'll lay over the covers."

Luke opened the window and pulled the curtain back. He looked over all the stalls in the parking lot, squinting at the shadows at what might have been lurking.

Nobody was outside.

———

LUKE TOLD ANITA he would meet her and the boys at the grocery store after work, but he took a detour to the 7-11 to buy another pack of cigarettes. He smoked one in the parking lot, breathing deep the calm of the nicotine. The feeling overwhelmed him, and then he looked at his watch.

He arrived at the grocery store breathless. The screams were the first thing he heard. They were identical screams, irritating and anxiety-inducing. Luke's lungs ached the closer he got to the cereal aisle, where Anita tried to pry at box from Andrew's hands. Oliver cried in a collapsed heap on the floor.

"Boys, I'm not going to buy either cereal if you can't behave," she said, putting the box back on the shelf. Andrew screamed and grabbed a new box, and Anita wiped her forehead and sighed.

Luke coughed as he approached. He pulled at his collar and tried to smell the smoke. His fingers shook, instincts driving him when his wife turned her head.

"Luke," she said. "Luke, where were you?"

"I'm sorry," Luke said. "I lost track of time."

Andrew grabbed at her legs and she bowed her head. "I'm going to lose it," she said. "The baby's giving me the worst heartburn and the boys have been with me with me all day." Her breath quivered. Her shaking fingers wrung tight around her grocery list. "They're sick of me."

Luke's balled his fist against his chest and tried not to cough. "I'm so sorry, Ani." He reached out and touched her shoulder.

"Just take them," she said, shrugging out of his grasp. "Just take them home and I can finish this."

"Are you sure?" he asked.

"Yes, I'm sure," she said. She put her list in the cart. Luke tried to look at her but she kept her head down. She ran her hand over her stomach and bit at her lip.

"Okay," he said.

He crouched down and picked Oliver off the floor. He grabbed Andrew's hand and lugged both his sons out of the store. They screamed and thrashed. They beat their kid fists against his flesh. He tried to be a good husband, a good father, but everyone in the grocery store glared at him when he passed.

Dragging the boys across the parking lot, Luke heard the sound of gears ticking, and he looked up to see the white BMX bike that lingered in his thoughts every night. The kid was on it, wearing baggy shorts and big headphones. He had no helmet and his long hair flipped behind him in the wind as he weaved his bike between all the cars.

Luke's grip tightened, but there was nothing he could do. He drew a breath, his chest burning, heart throbbing, erratic. He crossed the parking lot, holding tight to his son's hands. He dragged them both to the car like heavy burdens.

———

AFTER WORK, Luke took off his safety helmet in front of the mirror. His usually tousled locks fell flat around his face.

He'd always been told that he had a great head of hair. He'd cut it shorter over the years, and Anita said that his conservative haircut suited him, that his hair was less distracting, that the short and shellacked style hardened his jawline. Despite her approval, Luke often thought back to the flyaway waves he'd sported when he first met her. He ran his fingers through the matted strands, tired and worn from another day of work.

He looked at himself in the mirror. He watched his jaw shift as he ground his teeth.

———

BASS RIFFS VIBRATED through the walls into the late night, each song more obnoxious than the last. Anita rolled onto her back and moaned.

"I can't stand those renters," she said.

"The guy's name is Blake Bennett."

"That's a terrible name," she said. She shifted and rubbed her hand over her chest.

"Heartburn again?" he asked.

She nodded and rolled onto her side again, turning her back to him. Her shoulders rose and sank with her deep breaths in the dark. Luke tried to unclench his jaw. He sat up and massaged Anita's shoulder, but she only responded with a whine of irritation that filled his own chest with tightness and ache. He climbed out of bed and pulled his clothes on. He went downstairs and put on his jacket with the cigarettes in the pocket. They shifted in the package against his heavy steps.

Luke rang the neighbour's doorbell and pounded at the door until Blake Bennett answered, wearing a wrinkled graphic shirt and faded plaid pajama pants. The pounding beats sifted out the open door.

"Yeah?" Blake asked, adjusting his plastic thick-rimmed glasses.

"Could you turn your music down?" Luke asked.

"What you got against my music, man?"

"I don't have anything against your music," Luke said. "It's just too loud. My wife's pregnant and she can't sleep, and I have to work in the morning, so—"

"Easy, man."

"I can't take it easy. Your music's coming through my wall."

"Okay, man."

Blake went to close the door, but Luke put his hand out.

"Look," Luke said, "I know you probably think that it's cool to do whatever you want, but your actions do affect other people."

Blake Bennett hesitated, his mouth open and gawked. "Okay," he said. "I'm gonna turn the music down. I didn't mean to piss you off."

"And you left your truck unlocked the other night," Luke added.

"Oh, really?" Blake asked. "I didn't even notice. Did you lock it or something?"

Luke's throat tightened. "Well, yeah," he said.

"That was nice of you, man. I'll have to remember to lock it next time, I guess."

"You probably should," Luke said.

Blake Bennett nodded and smiled. He closed the door. The music fell silent, but Luke didn't feel any sense of accomplishment. He headed back to his front door, his fists clenching, his chest still pounding. He noticed that the kid's truck was still unlocked. Luke considered taking something from inside, but he dug into his pocket and pulled out a cigarette instead. He smoked it in the shadows and felt better.

———

Anita put the dishes away after dinner and Luke helped her clean the table. She handed him a damp rag.

"I was reading about you sweating at night," Anita said.

"It's nothing, Ani," Luke said.

"I read that it might have something to do with low-testosterone levels," she said.

"What?"

She studied him for too long. He had to look away. He looked down at the table, the white heat rings, the scratches. There were new lines, permanent marker lines. He scrubbed at them but he couldn't get the stains out of the oak.

"It's getting worse," she said. "You sweat practically every night."

"I'm fine," he said.

He grit his teeth and wiped at the marker lines, black lines, bleeding lines.

"Luke?" Anita asked.

He threw the rag down. "What are these goddamn marks on the table?"

"It's okay, Luke." She walked to him, put her arms around his shoulders. She ran her hand down his chest. "The boys were making you cards for Father's Day," she said.

"Well they kind of ruined the table."

"You know they didn't mean it," she said. "It was my fault. I should have paid more attention."

He bit his tongue and sighed. He ran his hand through his limp weak hair.

She leaned in and kissed his neck. "They got you an air freshener for your car," she said, laughing. "They said it smells like the pulp mill."

———

Blake Bennett was washing his truck in the driveway when Luke got home from work. Luke pulled the groceries from his car and walked up.

"You know, you forgot to lock your truck again," Luke said.

"I forget all the time," Blake said. "Half the time I don't even lock the house when I leave."

"Are you serious?" Luke asked. "You know there's a kid that comes round here to steal shit, right?"

"What?"

"I left a slip in your mail box a couple weeks ago."

"I don't remember seeing it, man." Blake twisted the hose nozzle to the pulse setting. Water beat against the side of the truck.

"You need to be responsible for your stuff," Luke said.

Blake shrugged. "If he goes through my car he's just gonna steal my CDs or whatever."

"Well, if that's what you want," Luke said. His pulse throbbed in his neck. He cleared his throat and felt himself reaching for his pack of cigarettes.

"I don't really give a shit about my CDs," the guy said.

Luke stared. His fingers shook as pulled out a cigarette and lit it. He inhaled deep. The burn filled his lungs and he held the cigarette loose between his fingers, the gentle wisps of smoke curling up in the air. Blake didn't seem to notice, but then Luke turned and saw Joe drive past. Joe waved and did a double take.

Luke waved, stirring the smoke that swirled around him. His heart pounded hard and heavy in the cage of his chest.

—————

HE WORKED ANOTHER DAY like a good provider, watched over the kids like a good father, helped clean the table like a good husband. He managed to sneak away before bed, managed to have a moment where he breathed in deep and let the smog fill his lungs. He showered at the end of the night and washed the smoke, soaped himself clean so he came out scented like the Old Spice body wash Anita always bought him. He dried his hair, brushed his teeth and climbed into bed beside his wife. She propped herself up beside him. She ran her fingers through his hair.

"I hope he has your hair," Anita said. "The boys got my hair. I'd love for a man in the family to carry on your lush head of hair." She smiled at him, rubbing her stomach.

"You don't know it's a boy," Luke said.

"Of course I do," she said. "Do you doubt me?" She looked up at him. She put her hand on his cheek.

He wondered what she saw when she looked at him, what she thought of him. He thought about all the times when he'd lie beside her when she was pregnant with the boys. She'd smell the smoke on his clothes, and she'd suggest that maybe things would be better if only he'd quit.

He swallowed. He could taste the nicotine. He leaned in and kissed her. He smelt her hair, breathed in her skin. He wanted to press his face against her chest and rest his head just for a little while. He drew a breath, drew in the coconut milk scent of her, but then she leaned into him. She curled into him, and he wrapped his arms around her and fought not to cling too hard.

"I love everything about you," she said.

Dread filled him, coiled tight and burning in his chest.

⸻

After work, Luke drove to 7-11 and hesitated before getting out of the car. He breathed in deep, breathed in the crisp clean air until its emptiness made him ache for new pack of smokes. He tore off the plastic wrap and opened the package, pulled out the first cigarette and lit it. The first one, but not the last. He leaned his head back against his seat and rolled the window down. He opened his mouth and tried to exhale circles, but he had never been that skilled.

He tried and tried but the end of the cigarette came too soon.

⸻

He got up early on Saturday morning, covered in sweat again. He went for a jog and came back relieved. The television kept the boys occupied in the living room. Anita brought out the outdoor cushions and took off the cover from the barbeque. Luke joined her on the patio. He offered to help her but she turned away.

"Heartburn again?" he asked.

She shook her head. "I can smell the smoke on you."

He bit his lip, felt his jaw clench tight.

"That's what you do when you get up at night," she said. "I thought I was just being sensitive the first time I smelt it."

His shoulders sank with his exhale. "I'm sorry," he said, gripping at the patio railing. He dug his nails against the chipping paint on the metal. "It just happened. I just slipped."

"Did you smoke in front of the boys?" she asked.

"No." He looked at her, looked for too long.

"You're supposed to tell me if something's bothering you."

Luke traced his fingers over the railing, felt the slopes in the chipped paint. "I'm just tired," he said.

"From what?" she asked. "Work?"

Luke shrugged. "It's everything, I guess."

"You were doing so well," Anita said.

"I know," Luke said.

"How much are you smoking now?"

"I don't know." Luke didn't want to look at her. "Two, maybe three a day."

Anita sighed. She leaned against the railing beside him, her fingers clutching, turning white. "You don't just pick up smoking after four years for nothing."

"You've never smoked, Ani. You have no idea what it's like."

"I know what you went through before," she said. "I'm your wife. I was there for you."

"You don't understand," he said. He pushed away and dragged his fingers through his hair. "I just needed time. I needed some relief."

"Relief from what?" she asked. "You've got a family, Luke."

She kept on saying it. She wasn't making it any easier, not with her hand on her stomach and the worried look on her face. Her eyes were glossy and she shared his gaze, the weakness in it. He had a half-finished pack in his pocket and all he wanted was to light one.

"It's that fucking kid," he said. "I hate that he's going around our complex, stealing shit out of cars. I work hard, Ani. Everything was fine until that kid started showing up."

She slid her hand across the railing. He felt the instinct to pull his hand away, but he waited for her to take it, her fingers curling around his palm. She leaned in and hugged him, but all he felt was her pregnant stomach keeping them apart.

———

He walked circles around the complex parking lot. He lingered in the shadows instead of lighting up. He clenched his fits at his sides instead of burying his hands in his pocket. Before he quit he smoked a pack a day. He only stopped because of the distractions.

He thought of Anita sleeping soundly. He thought of the boys adjusting to a shared bedroom again. He thought about Father's Day. He thought about becoming a father again. He fidgeted, dug in his jacket pocket. His fingers flinched around the pack of cigarettes and he wondered what the real distraction was.

He walked back to his doorstep and that was when he caught the flash of white, the noises behind the neighbour's truck. The kid was there, flashlight in hand, pushing his uncoiled wire hanger between the window and the door.

Luke hesitated, his lungs burning. He dropped his lighter, his smokes, his devil's sticks scattering on the pavement. The kid looked up as Luke approached. Luke shouted and the kid bolted for his bike. He dropped his flashlight and climbed on, pedalling.

Luke sprinted, reaching out to grab the sleeve of the kid's sweatshirt. He tripped over the bike, tumbling over it and the kid. He grabbed the kid and pinned him to the ground, gasping, his fists clenching, the kid's face a distorted blur in the dark.

"Stay out of my neighbourhood," Luke said.

"Fuck you," the kid said.

Balling the sweatshirt in his hand, Luke lifted his arm and threw a punch at the kid's gawking face. The kid moaned. The kid squirmed.

Luke threw another punch, his wrist locked, knuckles aching. The burn in his lungs filtered down through his arm and into his fist. His knuckles came back with blood and Luke clenched his fist tighter. He threw punches, one after the other, again and again. He breathed in the night air, thick and heavy, filling his lungs until he was heaving over the kid's face.

"Stay the fuck out of my neighbourhood, you little fucking piece of shit."

Lights flickered around him. He heard windows opening, heard the neighbours gasp. He looked up. Joe's bedroom light was on, his shadow in the window. Blake Bennett stood on the lawn in his plaid pajama pants.

He heard the kid moan underneath him, and then he heard his wife calling his name.

Anita ran to him in her slippers and her robe, her hand over her stomach. Her voice wavered. She asked him what he was doing. She begged him to stop. In the flickering light, he saw that her eyes were wet.

He tried to inhale but he couldn't breathe deep enough.

"IT'S FUNNY TO THINK OF IT," HE SAID, "WHAT REALLY SCARES YOU GIRLS."

THINSPIRATION

He seemed normal at first, a middle-aged man, tall, built, bearded. He walked up to the car and asked me for a cigarette. I reached for the pack on the dashboard and dug inside for my last slender stick. When I turned back he had a gun pointed at my face.

"Get into the passenger seat," he said.

His steady grasp took control of the moment, knuckles bent tight around the grip, his index finger pressed firm over the trigger. I tried to draw a breath but my lungs sat like decaying remains in my chest. My hands started to shake. The frail cigarette slipped through my fingers and rolled under the seat.

"C'mon now," he said. "Unbuckle your belt and slide over." The skin of his neck strained tight against his swallow. He waited; tense seconds passing as his gaze drifted from my face and moved slowly over my frame.

I slipped back against my seat, lightheaded, the taste of ashes filling my mouth.

Beyond the vehicle there was laughing, sounds of a family on the other side of the rest stop parking lot, unloading their SUV with picnic supplies, pop, chips and hot dogs. They were all too preoccupied to notice my situation. I drew another cigarette breath, my gag-reflex straining as I reached to unbuckle my seat belt.

"There we go," he said. "Move over now. Come on."

I climbed over the gear shift and sidled into the passenger seat. He unlocked the door and climbed in, his scent filling the car, the aroma of diner breakfasts, of maple syrup and sausages, sweat, exhaustion and rage. He ran his fingers through his hair and turned the key in the ignition. The engine rumbled alive, shaking the empty space in my stomach. I shut my eyes and tensed my grip over my knees, thinking of pleasant thoughts, of fantasy, images of pretty girls who'd persevered.

"What are you going to do?" I asked.

"You'll still get to go wherever you're going," he said. "I'm just going to do the driving until I get to where I need to be. Then you can have your car back." He looked at me, staring intently. "You're going to be good, right?"

I nodded.

"No protesting, no nothing."

"No," I said.

"That's what I like to hear." He tucked the gun beside the seat, put the car into gear and pulled out onto the highway.

He drove the speed limit with his thick fingers clenched tight around the wheel. He stared at the road, eyes straight ahead, determined. My gaze shifted to the window. I stared at nothing but the passing blur of sights, open fields of vegetation, just an endless mass of green. I thought about opening the door, about jumping, but then I caught my reflection in the side mirror. My pale face reflected the glare of the sun. I turned my cheek and studied my jaw, lifted my hand and pulled the skin taut.

"What are you doing all the way out here?" he asked. "Girls your age shouldn't travel alone."

I pressed my fingers under my chin, wrapped my thumb around the tendons in my neck and gripped tight, model-steady. I met my own gaze and still couldn't recognize myself, my gaunt cheeks more ghostly than glowing, my pale lips unable to smile.

"You a runaway?" he asked. "You trying to start a better life somewhere else?"

I shook my head. "Not really."

He breathed a laugh and loosened his grip. He let his fingers relax over the wheel.

"It's funny how easy it is," he said. "The last girl thought I was gonna rape her. She kept on pleading with me. I didn't even have to rely on my gun. Made it so much easier to drive."

My fingers twitched over my throat. I swallowed. My esophagus burned. The taste of orange juice and bile still lingered in my mouth. It was the reason why I'd pulled into the rest stop to begin with, was to purge the mistakes I'd made, to cleanse myself of my lack of control. I thought of the family and their picnic lunch, their smiles wide, more like grimaces.

It wasn't often, but at times I could be realistic about my situation.

"It's funny to think of it," he said, "what really scares you girls."

The wide neckline of my shirt slipped off my shoulder when I shrugged. I reached to pull the sleeve back up, wrapped my arms tight around my chest.

He turned the radio on but he couldn't pick up any stations. He left it on anyway, filling the car with whir and static, the sound of salt water lapping against a shore. I eyed the open emptiness of the sky, felt the heat burning my cheeks. Thoughts trickled into my head, fantasies of starving on a remote beach in the sun.

He drove for an hour with his hand on the gear shift and the gun still tucked between us. The black metal caught bleak reflections of the sun's glare, heated tension that burned the empty pit of my stomach.

The growls sounded loud, filled the car.

He looked me over again, eyed me for too long. Goosebumps pimpled my skin. I pressed my knees together, grasped my hands underneath my thighs, palms slipping under the heat, the sweat, the unease. He studied my posture, his gaze drifting again, all the way down to my bare legs. I winced and gathered a breath.

"Please stop," I said. "Just look at the road." He wrinkled his brows and turned away.

I felt like I was going to shatter, but all I did was flinch when he geared down and turned onto the next exit, the sign beside it listing all the nearest shops and restaurants in the next town.

"You got money?" he asked.

"Why?"

"I haven't eaten in a while," he said.

He didn't see me shake my head. I sat up straight in my seat, sucked in my empty gut, my reflection in the mirror rigid and tense. My chest pounded at the thought of seeing him eat, seeing his teeth sink into fleshy meat, thick grisly fat right down to the bone.

He pulled up to the McDonald's drive-thru. The line-up was long, an intestine string of cars leading to the window that expelled paper bags full of grease. He groaned and glanced over at me, the shrunken shifty mess that I was in the passenger seat. He reached over and pushed down the lock on my door.

"What do you want?" he asked.

"I don't need anything," I said.

"Sure you do," he said, studying my arms, my thighs, my stomach. "There's still a ways to go," he said. "I'm not going to stop again."

"I'm fine," I said.

"Are you?" he asked.

I nodded, stomach aching, begging.

His throat tensed again. He bit his lip and breathed heavily, his fingers slipping from the steering wheel. He made fists, clenched them tight before he turned to me, stare piercing in black, worse than his gun.

"Where's your purse?" he asked. "Where's your money?"

I hesitated, mouth turning dry as he turned and dug into the pile of clothes and magazines and makeup in the back of the car. He grabbed the strap of my open satchel and pulled the bag onto his lap. I flinched when he dug out my journal. He flipped it open and revealed it all, the textbook of inspiration that kept me so empty inside.

He flipped through the pages full of magazine clippings and journal entries. The numbers at the top of each page started at the weight I used to be and counted backward in awkward increments, my hard abrasive handwriting highlighting my journey of self-loathing. He stopped on the last entry, where I'd tucked that picture of Kiera Knightly I'd cut out from an issue of *Vogue*. In it she was sitting in a white dress, sitting before a typewriter. She looked so dreamy, so romantic, so at ease.

"It's just a picture I like," I said.

"What do you like about it?" he asked.

The radio static still filled the car. I tried to concentrate on it but the sound wasn't calming anymore. "I think she's pretty," I said.

He looked down at the photo. "She looks like a sheet of drywall with a face."

I squeezed at my thighs, the meaty middle parts that flattened against the seat, spreading out like pancake batter. Bile brimmed up my throat, the taste of ugly truths.

"She has it better than I do," I said.

He stared at me, dark pupils reflecting my face.

The car behind us honked and he tossed the journal at me. The picture slipped between my legs and to the floor. I reached to pick it up.

"Sit back." He handed me my satchel, demanded me to dig out some money.

I handed him my last ten dollars and shifted back, breathing deep as I let myself crumble into the curve of my seat. I glanced at the mirror and blinked, tried to make my gaze look real, responsive.

He drove up to the drive-thru speaker and ordered two cheeseburgers and a large coke.

My chest started throbbing. The tears burned behind my eyes.

He paid for the food at the window and set the brown paper bag beside his gun. He drove to the back of the parking lot. He killed the engine. The rumbling gone, it was just the sound of his breathing, the sound of my own stomach growling, the scent of his presence, cigarettes and sweat and grime. Exhaustion. He dug one of the burgers from the bag and handed it to me.

"I'm not hungry," I said.

"You should eat anyway," he said. "It's still going to be a few hours."

I shook my head, staring at the burger, still wrapped in its greasy waxed paper. "I can't," I said. "It's going to ruin everything."

He unwrapped the burger and grabbed my wrist, forced me to hold the flimsy bun in my grasp. "Eat it," he said.

I shook my head.

He leaned over the gear shift, his steady grasp bearing down, taking control. "I'm the fucking kidnapper here. You're going to do what I say."

"Please," I said. "You can take the car. You can have whatever you want. Please."

He tightened his grasp. He dug his fingers deep, pressed at my triggers.

"You don't even know me," I said, straining. I winced and writhed, moans drifting from my throat as I tried to pry myself away. My grasp tensed around the burger. Cheese brimmed from the edges of the bun. The cooked meat showed through the cracks, seeping clear grease like tears. I pressed my lips together, tried to resist the calling groan of my stomach. He gripped my wrist tighter, lifted the food to my face.

"Take a fucking bite," he said.

It wasn't until then that I started crying.

"IT'S LIKE EVERY PUZZLE IS ITS OWN APOCALYPSE. NO PEOPLE. JUST SCENERY."

BETTER PLACES

t's been sunny ever since the dead started walking. They get clos-er with every sunrise, their groans a chasing echo on the high-way. I've been riding this bike for days with my weight leaning over the handlebars, feet slipping off the pedals, breath heaving, weak, dehydrated, gravity taking hold.

There's a dishevelled bed and breakfast off the road, its windows boarded. The zombies approach and I stumble off my bike and run. I round the building. I pry at the boards, bloodying my fingers until there's a crawl space big enough to climb through. Inside, the front lobby is littered with the fragmented wood of a demolished staircase. A rope hangs from the second floor and I struggle to pull myself up.

There's a man on the landing pointing a gun.

He says, "This isn't your property."

"There's nowhere else to go," I say, collapsing on the floor, plead-ing. "You have to help me."

His fingers flinch over the trigger. "You think I care what happens to you?"

"Please," I say. "I lost my apartment. Looters broke into the build-ing and took everything. They would have killed me if I hadn't run." The words shudder up my throat and I blink, eyes stinging and hot. "I haven't eaten in days."

His gaze drifts away from mine. He looks me over. He runs his tongue along his bottom lip and he says, "You can suck my dick if you want."

He steps forward, his eyes dark. I crawl back, looking down the open landing below. Outside, the zombies pound against the boards, the sound throbbing with my chest.

"I haven't even seen a woman in months," he says. "What else could you possibly do for me?"

I shake my head. He takes another step, closing in, towering over me.

He says, "You can either give me a blowjob or I can kick you back down there."

He says, "Come on," and he unzips his fly.

He says, "This is about survival, not your fucking dignity."

He leans against the wall and pulls his dick out. He smiles when I crawl to him. His lap of pubic hair smells of sour sweat and piss. I hold my breath and close my mouth over his hard warmth. He wraps his hand around the back of my head. He presses the cold metal of the gun against my scalp and he says, "Put in some effort."

I try not to retch.

───

HE WAS PREPARED.

He spends all his time in the solarium on the third floor. It used to be the breakfast room but now it's his domain. He has crates of canned food and bottled water. He has guns and crowbars and knives. He has jigsaw puzzles on every table, a collection of different places, better places: The Eiffel Tower, Niagara Falls—the Venetian Canal.

He says, "You've got to have something to do."

He opens a can of beans and sits at the table with a half-finished puzzle on top. The picture on the box is of a historical park in Thailand, a grey bell tower monument before a river of lily pads and pink flowers. Everything is bright, alive.

He says, "It's like every puzzle is its own apocalypse. No people. Just scenery."

He hands me the can of beans and I take a bite. All I can taste is him. He asks, "What's your name?"

I tell him. He smiles and I pass the can back.

"I haven't talked to a woman since this all started," he says, spooning the beans into his mouth. "All I ever see out there is zombies and bandits. You're like a unicorn."

My fingers flinch over the puzzle pieces.

"Do you really want to stay here?" he asks.

I look at him, his gaze the first human one I've seen in days.

He says, "You don't have much of a choice, do you?"

His voice is gentle, but my stomach tightens at the sound of his masculine tone. He slides the can across the table and I stare at the beans, little organs floating in red.

He says, "Don't worry. Judah will take care of you."

———

THE GRIT ON HIS SHEETS rubs against my skin.

He tosses and turns in the dark, his presence warm beside me. He reaches across the bed and grabs my wrist. My muscles tense.

"Take your clothes off," he says.

"No, please."

He climbs over me, his darkness heavy. His hair hangs in sweaty strings over my face. He slips his fingers under my shirt. A whimper shakes up my throat as he forces my arms through the sleeves. I moan, but he covers my mouth.

He says, "You don't want them to hear you, do you?"

He presses his hand down the front of my jeans. He yanks them down, pries them off my ankles before he shoves me back.

He says, "Spread your fucking legs." He looms over me, waits until I open up, and he rubs there, rough fingers in my folds, pushing in. My shaking, he likes it. He gets hard. He forces himself on me.

He says, "Stop crying."

I bite my lip, wincing when he pulls my knees around his waist.

The mattress creaks and his laboured grunts echo in the empty room. I distract myself by thinking of the zombies. When he comes, his groan sounds just like them.

⸻

It's barely dawn and the sound of motorcycles echoes outside, spit sizzling on hot pavement. Judah jolts from the bed. He grabs his gun from the nightstand and tucks it into the waist of his jeans.

Glass shatters in another room. Heavy footsteps echo through the halls. This was how my apartment was lost. Looters. Bandits. Men in leather, with aggression, more agile than the undead.

I pull the sheets around me. My limbs stiffen. Judah picks up the crowbar beside the bed. He grabs my wrist and drags me behind him just as the bandits tear into the room. Judah pummels the first with the flat side of the crowbar. Then he pulls out the gun, cocks it. The second bandit backs away, holding his jagged metal pipe raised. He's young, blonde, and he screams, "What you got, faggot!"

Judah points the gun, finger on the trigger. "I've got a whole lot more than you," he says.

The blonde holds his arms up, pushes his chest out. "Go ahead," he says. "You'll have a hell of a time disposing of my corpse out there, shithead."

Judah tenses.

The bandit on the floor heaves. He grasps the edge of the table with the Thailand puzzle and he pulls himself up. He staggers back, his gaze falling on me.

"Do you want to fuck her?" Judah asks. "You wanna fuck my bitch? You're not looting any of my shit, but you can fuck her and then you can leave."

The blonde bandit says, "What?"

The gasping bandit hesitates, staring stupid, struggling to take a breath. "You fucking serious, dude?" he asks.

I look at Judah and his face is expressionless, empty. A tightness burns through my chest. I shake my head. My eyes are hot, wet, stinging.

Judah says, "Do it."

"No."

"Let them see you." He kicks me forward. I turn back to look at him but he points the gun at my face. "Serve our guests," he says. He grabs the sheet and pries it out of my grasp.

The bandits take turns.

The blonde bends me over a puzzle of the Eiffel Tower, the pieces sticking to my chest, crumbling. Then the second bandit shoves me back on the Empire State, the force of his thrusts tearing the building apart. The blonde joins in, pulls my head over the edge of the table, forces my mouth around his dick so I'm fucked both ways in the rubble.

They leave satisfied, calm, and it's not until their motorcycles grunt outside that I gather my breath and slide off the table.

Judah looks up from Thailand. He's already opened another can of beans.

He says, "You saved us. You did your part."

———

THE BANDITS COME BACK. They want more. They empty their back-packs of luxuries: toothbrushes and mouthwash and razors.

Judah smiles and says, "Sure, do whatever you want with her."

He shaves while the bandits ride me. They take out their aggression on my flesh, hitting my face, my ass, my tits. Then they leave, burning heat on the pavement, spit and semen on my face. Judah cups my chin in his hands, his face fresh, smelling of aftershave, his new gaze darker, taking ownership.

He pushes me on top of Thailand. He's got a bottle of perfume, the glass cut like a diamond. He holds it up and he sprays the delicate pink fragrance in my face.

He says, "You smell like a unicorn now."

———

MORE MEN, different men. The word spreads and I get taken over and over again.

The apocalypse isn't about the zombies. The men bring liquor and cigarettes and luxury and Judah gets all primped up while I get fucked in the Swiss Alps, in the Mayan Rivera, in the middle of Westminster Abbey.

The space between my legs is a dull ache. My tits are darkened with bruises. My throat's hoarse, rubbed raw. The solarium is littered with puzzle pieces, the world a wreck.

At night Judah dresses in his new silk bathrobe. He takes me to Thailand and says, "There's no better place than here."

He always gets his turn.

He says, "You couldn't do this alone."

He says, "Without me, you'd just be a dead little unicorn."

He says, "Say you're my little unicorn. Say it."

Survival.

———

THE NEXT TIME the bandits come, one of them spits on my asshole and shoves his dick inside. The tight ache winds into my stomach. All I do is scream. Afterwards, Judah sits beside me on the mattress. He strokes my hair and I wipe my tears on the lapel of his robe.

He wraps a sheet around me. We eat canned beef ravioli paired with vintage Chianti and we put Thailand back together. He works on the land and the sky and asks me to piece together the lilies and the water. I have to lean forward because it hurts too much to sit.

He says, "The next time you scream, I'll fuck you with my crowbar while holding a plastic bag over your head."

"I'm sorry," I say.

I fit together two pieces, the biggest pink flower in the river.

———

ALL THE RETURNING VISITORS attract the attention of the undead.

Judah's got his fingers in my ass, teaching me how to take it without crying. Over my whimpers is the sound of pounding, undead hands on the boarded windows downstairs.

He says, "You moan too much. They probably heard you."

He brings his crowbar outside and he kills the zombies in his bathrobe, standing back so he can take them out one by one, swinging the bar at their faces, taking them to the ground. He stands over them, defiant, driving curved titanium teeth into flesh and bone. The sound of the cracking vibrates through the window.

Judah returns angry, his chest heaving, blood splatter all over his robe. He takes it off and holds it up, shaking the stained silk in my face.

He says, "You're going to get me a new one."

It's all my fault. I'm a bad little unicorn, bent over Thailand. He punishes me, forces his whole fist up my backside.

———

THE SUNLIGHT BEAMS IN through the solarium windows. Outside there's groaning.

Judah's asleep in his new plaid flannel robe. It's not as nice, but I did my best.

He says I can do better.

I spray perfume on my neck. I smell like magical lilies in spring water and I tiptoe down the hallway with a crowbar and a switchblade hung from a string around my neck. I climb down the rope and stand outside for the first time since earning my survival.

Goosebumps form as the breeze hits my naked flesh.

The switchblade hangs between my breasts, bobs with my chest, my aching heartbeat.

There's a lone zombie, a former male with a dead gaze, his arms outstretched, wanting me. His footsteps waver over the uneven ground as he approaches. He groans, makes it so easy to lift the bar up, to let everything out because he sounds just like all the grunting men.

I pry hunks of flesh from his face, one swing at a time. I knock him over, mashing his skull into a red mess, kidney beans and lukewarm beef ravioli in tomato sauce. Then I open the switchblade and I cut through the meat, digging in deep, covering the knife with blood and infection, Chianti red.

I fold up the knife and I take it with me, tucking the streaked metal underneath my pile of collected river pieces. Water and lilium.

———

I CAN DO BETTER.

Judah gets out of bed and pushes me back on the table. I wrap my legs around him. I dig into my pile of puzzle pieces. I wrap my arms around his broad shoulders and I hold him close. He fucks me hard, too preoccupied to notice the knife clutched tight in my grasp, too preoccupied to feel when I cut through the flannel and into his flesh.

He says, "You love it when I ride you in Thailand, don't you, little unicorn?"

I tell him, "Yes, I love it. I love it. I love it."

———

WE REBUILD THAILAND.

I finish the river. All the pieces are sticky with bodily fluids, blood and semen and sweat. Across the table, Judah reaches behind him, trying to scratch his back. He winces and unties the sash of his robe. He stands and takes it off, taking notice of the stain, the circle of red on the back. His finger slips through the slit in the fabric.

He looks at me.

He doesn't say anything because it's too late.

My toes curl as he sits down. He bites his lip and he picks up another piece of the puzzle. It's a part of the bell monument, a piece of grey brick. His fingers start to shake as he tries to fit the piece in place. The vein in his neck throbs. His face goes red. He exhales, heavy. He makes a fist and pounds the table, shoves the puzzle at me, the pieces flying. He knocks the table over.

"You cunt! You fucking cunt!"

He smacks my face and tackles me to the floor. He snatches my wrists and he holds me down, his shaking grasp vibrating through me.

"I'm going to eat you," he says. "I'm going to fucking devour you! I'm going to chew your fucking snatch off, you fucking shit whore!"

I writhe out of his grasp, crawling to the mattress, reaching for the nightstand where his gun is. The trigger is cold and hard. He grabs my ankle, digs his nails into my skin. I groan and turn over, aiming the barrel. My finger tightens and a deafening bang fills the room, making a hole in his shoulder, red filling in, spreading.

His groan echoes loud, guttural. A male cry.

He says, "I fucking saved you." He groans and heaves, showing his pain, gritting his teeth. "I protected you. You'd just be another dead little bitch out on that highway if it wasn't for me."

I shoot him again, this time in the knee. He starts heaving. His breaths become moans. His body shakes when he tries to stand, but I grab his crowbar and I swing it against his forehead. He falls face down, letting out one hopeless moan before his head hits the floor.

It takes all day for him to turn. I finish Thailand while I wait, fitting together the soggy pieces while he shifts and shudders, his skin fading to a bruised shade of grey. His lips purse and sputter nonsense.

Bitch. Cunt. Whore. Unicorn.

He comes to and breaks into a fever sweat, his forehead greasy, hair hanging in strings down his face. He moans, chokes up vomit, and it spreads; a bile yellow river, the puzzle pieces floating like lily pads.

He tries to stand but his limbs are stiff.

I fill a backpack with canned food and bottled water. He watches me get dressed.

He says, "You'll die out there. You can't survive on your own." He groans and lifts his head, the vomit trickling off the sweaty ringlets of his hair.

I pick up the crowbar and I stand over him.

He's still human, his gaze still dark, still angry. He says, "Not yet."

He tries to say my name but it just sounds like he's coming. His groan fills the room and I swing the crowbar over his head, cracking his skull, making a hole big enough to fuck him. I dig deep, chipping at the bone until his groan drowns in sick. It's just like beating the other zombie, only Judah's dead gaze has humanity. I take it from him. I cut it from him. I gut his stomach. I flood the floor with his gall.

The heat burns in my lungs and I heave. The tears streak down my cheeks, flushing my dry skin hot.

———

MY BIKE'S STILL where I left it. I pedal out into the summer heat. There are zombies on the horizon, walking in the sunset like strewn puzzle pieces. The highway's quiet and long.

There's no better place than here.

BEHIND EACH PICTURE IS
A PRISTINE PATCH OF LILAC
PAINT, A SLIGHTLY DARKER
SHADE THAN THE ONE
I THOUGHT MY WALLS
WERE ALL THIS TIME

HISTORICAL HOTTIES

M r. Allen announces the final assignment for our unit on World War II. He uses the words "poster project" and "pairs" and I sit stalling as the rest of the class shuffles around my desk. They're all buddies and best friends, already making decisions, already writing their names on the board at the front of the class.

I take one look over at Mr. Allen, thinking maybe he'll let me do this one alone for once, but he doesn't make eye contact, doesn't pay me any attention. Laughter erupts around me, that of excited plans and ideas. I pick up my textbook, adrenaline rushed and frantic.

I turn in my seat and glance over at Zoey, always scrawling indifference at the back of the class. She's drawing swastikas in her agenda, her head down, black fringe shifting as she scribbles. Her veil of hair covers her expression, but she digs her pen into the page, her fingertips whitened with her hardened grasp. I approach her desk, reminding myself that she needs a partner just as badly as I do. It's not until I sigh in front of her that she glances up from her agenda.

"Hey," I say, projecting casual, trying to soften my posture against the hard surface of my book. "I was just wondering if maybe you'd want to do this together."

She closes the agenda and leans back in her seat.

"There's really nobody else left in the class," I say.

She glances out at all the pairs with a grimace.

"Yeah," she says. "I guess there isn't much choice." She looks at me and smiles before retracing the lines of the swastika, sinking its shape even deeper into the pages. "I don't wanna do Hitler, though," she says. "Hitler's too obvious. Everybody's gonna do Hitler."

"We could do Joseph Stalin," I say.

"Yeah, sure," she says. "I don't know a lot about him, though."

"I do," I say. "My dad has a bunch of books about him."

She looks up.

"He's really interested in history, like wars and stuff." My voice drops and I resist the urge to bite my lip over her lack of a response. "We won't even have to use the library."

"We can't do the project at my house, though," she says. "My mom hates it when I have people over. Just give me your address." She hands me her red pen and pushes her agenda across the desk.

I click on the end and write between all the swastikas.

———

I CONSIDER TAKING DOWN the pictures above my bed before Zoey comes over, but she arrives before I'm able to, and I bring her up to my room, with its lilac walls and white antique furniture and floral covers. My plush bunny rabbit still sits atop my pillow. She looks at it all but doesn't scowl.

"Your room could be like totally Gothic in a southern kind of way," she says. "You should paint your walls a darker colour. Like mauve, or even just a darker purple."

"I don't know." I say. "It's always been this colour."

"You should," she says. "I'd totally kill for this room."

"My mom decorated it," I say. "She'd probably get mad if I changed anything."

"That sucks," she says. "It's not like it's even her room." She lets her backpack slip off her shoulder and takes a seat on my white canopy bed. She runs her hand over the floral quilt and leans over to pick up the plush bunny rabbit on my pillow.

"I've had that since I was a baby," I say.

"Oh yeah," she says, poking at the rabbit's plastic eyes. She drops her backpack on the floor and nods at the black and white photos of the men above my bed. "Are those, like, relatives of yours?" she asks.

"No," I say. "They're historical figures."

"Why are they on your wall?"

"I don't know," I say. "They're people I admire."

"You don't admire normal guys? Like singers and actors?"

"Not really," I say, hesitating. "I just like these pictures more. There's a story behind each person. It's kind of nice to think about sometimes."

I climb on the bed and point to the nearest photo. "See, this is Ernest Hemingway when he served in World War I. He was pretty cute, right?"

"I don't know," she says, shrugging. She runs her hand over her black fringe as she gazes over the other photos.

"That one's a postage stamp image of Nathan Hale," I say. "He was the world's first spy during the American Revolutionary War, but then the British caught him and hung him."

"Sucks for him," she says, studying the other photos before reaching up and pointing. "What about him? What's his deal?"

"That's Nicola Tesla," I say, waiting for her to recognize the name.

"I like his gaze," she says. "It's kind of seductive, like he's going to buy you a drink or something."

"I guess," I say. "He was an inventor, though."

"Sometimes I forget that you're like, super smart."

"Is there something wrong with that?" I ask.

"No," she says. "It's kind of cool, actually, that you're only into dudes who are dead." She takes a seat on the bed, digs into her backpack and pulls out her notebooks. They're all covered with upside down crosses and pentagrams and sayings penned by her aggressive hand.

The death of one is a tragedy. The death of millions is statistic.

"That's totally a Stalin quote," I say.

"What?" she asks. "It's a lyric from a song."

"Well, Stalin said it. It's in one of my books."

"Seriously?" she asks.

I pick up all the books I've pulled from Dad's shelf and I plop them down on the bed beside Zoey. She lifts a coffee table book about Stalin onto her lap and flips through the pages.

"So, your dad made you read about history when you were a kid?"

"He didn't make me," I say. She stares at me, waits for me to continue but all I feel is insecurity building up inside. "We used to go to the bookstore every weekend. He was mostly interested in the world wars, military sort of stuff."

She looks back down and flips through the pictures, Stalin in full uniform, moustached, with a hint of a smile on his lips.

"That's kind of cool," she says. "My mom used to read to me, but it was just like fairy tales and stuff like that. When I got older it just got kind of lame."

"Well, you can draw and get the poster board and be in charge of the layout," I say. "My dad pretty much taught me everything about Joseph Stalin, so there's no way we can't get an A on this."

She looks up from the page, tucks her long straight locks of black hair behind her ear and smiles. "Okay, cool."

———

ZOEY LEAVES JUST BEFORE Dad comes home in his coveralls, greasy blue and smelling of oil and exhaust fumes. He puts his lunch box on the table and climbs upstairs to shower and change. He returns and sits at his spot at the head of the table, looking so much smaller without the dirty loose-fitting uniform over his small frame.

Mom sets a trivet on the table and covers it with a hot pan of beef stroganoff out of a box. She used to make real stroganoff with fresh beef and sliced mushrooms, but it's just not something she does anymore, not with her new job stocking shelves at the drug store.

"What's the project on?" Dad asks.

"Joseph Stalin," I say.

"You know I still have those books in the basement..."

"I got them," I say.

"I just hope that Zoey girl doesn't take advantage of you," Mom says, picking up my plate, serving for me.

I sigh. "She won't, Mom. She's just quiet. She's not even that bad."

"I've always hated the idea of group projects," she says. "It's really not fair to the students who actually try to take things seriously. It's not fair to you if she does nothing and still ends up with your grade."

"It'll be fine, Mom." I say, picking up my fork, clutching it tight in my hand. "She came over, didn't she? We worked for like, two hours before Dad came home."

"You just need to stand up for yourself, Peyton. I don't want this ending up like the last time you had one of these group projects."

I grip my fork tighter.

Dad looks up, and shares a look with me before turning back to Mom. "Nothing's happened yet, Nora," he says. "Peyton's a smart girl. She knows what she's doing."

"It's fine, Dad," I say, stabbing my fork into the ground beef, breaking it up. My fingers are white and I try to loosen my grasp.

Mom takes a seat and sighs. Dad reaches out, pats her knee, but she shakes her head and reaches for the serving spoon.

———

MOM AND DAD ARGUE about all kinds of things before bed. Their voices always sound the same through the wall that separates their room from mine. Dad's tone radiates a casual calm that can never sway Mom's frantic emotional-based logic.

"I was surprised they even got along," Mom says.

"You know kids these days. They go through phases."

Mom sighs. "I know what girls are like, Daniel," she says.

"You're not giving her enough credit. Peyton's always been herself."

"She has," Mom says, "but she's growing up. Some of these girls are a bad influence."

I pull away from the wall, limbs tightening as I glance up at the men posted there, men Dad introduced me to, men he said were worth knowing about, men with pasts and stories and allure. I stare up at a photo of a Wilfred Owen, somber and sophisticated and clean-shaven, and I try to picture what his voice might sound like whispering poetics in my ear: *Beauty is yours and you have mastery, Wisdom is mine and I have mystery.*

"She could use a few friends, Nora," Dad says. "She's not going to dye her hair black just because of some girl."

I swallow and shift my gaze to the face of a twenty-year-old Johannes Brahms, so full of charm with his arms crossed in a fitted suit jacket, with a boyish pale face and swept locks of light hair. I picture his skilled composer fingers working over the piano keys, working over me.

"You just know her so well, don't you?" Mom asks.

"Nora, please."

"She's not a little girl," Mom says. "She's not going to side with you forever."

I fall back in bed and roll onto my side, hand between my legs, pressing my head against my pillow, folding its feathered weight over my ears so I can ignore them like I have so many times before. Still, Dad's voice penetrates through the wall.

"She's a smart girl," he says.

"Enjoy it," Mom says. "I mean it, Daniel. Enjoy it while it lasts."

———

ZOEY OPENS HER BINDER in class and she shows me all the photos she's printed. She arranges them over her desk, smiling, eager, excited the same way I used to be.

"I don't know why, but all the guys I'm into are like, totally evil," she says, pushing a photo of Lewis Powell across the desk. It's the one taken after he was arrested for conspiring to kill the president. He looks so rogue and uncaring, sitting against the cold black wall, hands bound in manacles, a man not worth the admiration, yet I study the photo and I imagine what his chest looks like under his tight sweater.

"He's probably my favourite," Zoey says. "He's got such a serious gaze."

"He used to scare me," I say, sliding the photo back in her direction. "I don't really know why—probably just because my dad used to emphasize how bad he was. I mean, he's only twenty-one here. Apparently he wasn't all that scared to die when they hung him."

"That's so sexy," Zoey says, eyes wide, excited. "I mean, what kind of guy would be like that these days?"

"I don't know," I say. "Not a lot."

"Most guys are like total pussies these days," she says. "At least he could look at death and accept what was coming."

I look back at the picture and swallow, thinking of the Stalin quote, thinking of my stuffed rabbit. For some reason I wonder what Zoey's stuffed bear looked like when she lost it.

She pushes another picture my way. "What about him?" she asks. "What do you think about him? His name's Leon something..."

"Leon Czolgosz," I say.

"Leon who?"

"Czolgosz," I say, slowing my pronunciation. "He assassinated President William McKinley in 1901. This is his mugshot."

"He's sexy too, in an older guy sort of way."

"Even though he actually killed someone?" I ask.

She shrugs. "I don't know. I guess it's bad but it's also what makes him hot."

"Did you do any research last night?" I ask.

"Not really," she says, gathering the pictures.

I haven't either, but I'm not yet willing to admit it.

———

There's a photo of a young Stalin in one of the books from the basement, taken in 1902 when he was twenty-three and smooth-faced, his hair effortlessly tousled in locks I can only imagine slipping my fingers though. He's in a dark jacket and a checkered shirt, bearing the slightest hint of a smile. I trace down the photo, admiring the slight curve of his lips, admiring his beard, so ruggedly handsome in a modern sort of way, his shadowed jawline and piercing stare barely a suggestion of the things he'd eventually be capable of doing.

I sit back against the bed and slip my hand between my thighs.

There's a knock on the door. I flinch and close the book just as Dad enters the room still in his coveralls, grease on his face.

"How's your project going?" he asks.

"Fine," I say. "I'm just taking notes."

He stands there and looks over my bed, smiling when he notices the coffee table book on Stalin. "I remember when we bought this one," he says, taking a seat on the bed. "It was the day after your seventh birthday." He flips to the inscription on the first page, purple pencil crayon in my sloppy kid printing: *This book belongs to Peyton and Daddy*. He holds it up and I force myself to smile.

"You went through such a war phase," he says. ""You said that you hated all the stories in your fairy tale books. Your mom used to get so angry. She thought you'd have nightmares about the Holocaust."

"Yeah," I say, forcing myself to laugh.

"We used to watch all those documentaries, too. Remember?"

"Uh huh," I say, shifting when he takes a seat on the bed. Back then he had a different job, one where he came home in a suit and tie and all he had to do was loosen it before reading to me, telling me I was so smart, telling me how lucky a father he was to have a daughter who had the same interests as him. Now he flips through the pages, getting to the one I was just looking at, the page with young Stalin. He puts his finger on the page, smudging Stalin's young gaze of accusation with his finger.

"Whoops," he says, looking down at his hands. "Sometimes I forget about all this." He rubs the oil on his knees, stands up and glances back at my quilt, where the oil's black stains from his uniform have transferred with the flowers. "Sorry," he says. "I can take it to the wash for you."

"It's okay," I say, wanting him to leave. "It's fine."

He smiles, looking down at the quilt and then back at me. I pull it up around me, waiting until Dad leaves and shuts the door behind him before I pull the book back onto my lap, sweeping my finger over Joseph's face before I slip my hand back under the blanket.

———

"My mom caught me smoking," Zoey says in class the next day. "I can't come over after school."

"What?" I ask.

"I wasn't even really smoking. She found a pack of cigarettes in my backpack. She couldn't even prove they were mine."

"My mom's like that," I say. "She always just assumes the worst."

"Oh my God," Zoey says. "Seriously, I just, I can never do anything to impress her. She never even gives me a chance. I tried telling her that I was going to your place to study and do research but she didn't even believe me. She thinks I'm so horrible, like all I ever do is hang out with people who are bad influences. It's not even easy to make friends with the right people. And they're never people she approves of."

My fingers slip over my notebook. Mom's voice rings in my head, the sound of paranoia, the fear of growing up. My heart beats heavy and I slip my fingers between the pages, pulling out the young Stalin picture I scanned for her the night before.

"Maybe this will lighten the mood," I say, smiling as I hand her the photo.

———

Joseph looks so suave, so handsome. I put him up on the wall, next to the men that Zoey and I spend all our time talking about. I put him next to my pillow and I lay in bed under my sheets, no quilt because it's in the wash.

I think about the stains. I think about Joseph Stalin, my lap buried under my sheets, fingers curled under the waist of my jeans while I imagine him leaning over the bank counter in Tiflis, his serious gaze confronting me, telling me that I'm a smart girl, that I know what to do, his hard Russian accent a lure that sinks deep into me, makes each breath hot in my lungs.

Footsteps sound outside the closed door. The knob turns. The hinges creak and Mom enters the room with my folded floral quilt draped over her arm. Her shriek echoes off the walls and she drops the quilt in the doorway.

"Get out!" I say.

She takes a step back, her eyes falling to the floor. She shields her gaze, her mouth gawked, feet frozen behind the quilt she just washed for me. I flinch and adjust the sheets, kicking my stuffed rabbit over the side of my bed.

"Your friend," she says. "You said your friend was coming over."

"She's grounded," I say.

Mom looks up, takes a breath. Her gaze falls on the wall; on the new men I've decided to put there, men I can't lie about. The heat's brimmed its way up, flushed my cheeks hot and awful, making me regret whatever desire it was I had to hang them up in the first place.

Mom's lips tighten. "You're supposed to be studying," she says.

"Get out," I say.

She blinks and her eyes go wide, but I hold my stare because there's nothing else I can say that will remove the attention I've already received.

"Get out of my room, Mom."

She just stands there. I bend down and pick the white rabbit from the floor. I throw it at her just as she turns, pulling the door over the quilt.

———

MOM AND DAD ARGUE in their room at night. I listen with my ear pressed to the wall.

"She was looking at those men," Mom says, her voice slipping into quiet.

"She's been hanging those pictures on her wall for years," Dad says.

"They're hanging over her bed, Daniel. She's fourteen. I know you've been ignoring it, that you don't want to admit what she's doing."

For a moment there is only the sound of my pounding heartbeat in my ears.

"Daniel," she says.

"I don't see how this is my fault," he says.

"You were the one who introduced her to all those men."

"That was years ago. I was educating her."

"Well, she clearly doesn't have the same fondness for those memories," she says.

There's a moment of silence and I cup my hands around my ear, straining to hear their voices.

Mom sighs. "She's just going to keep distancing herself if you don't talk to her."

"No. I, I can't. I can't talk to her about that."

"It doesn't even shock you that she's got a picture of Joseph Stalin above her bed?"

No response.

"I ignored those pictures at first, but Joseph Stalin? That's who she's thinks about when she..."

I swallow, feeling my pulse in my throat, lungs tight in my chest, white heat going to burst.

"Just talk to her," Mom says. "Tell her something. She's supposed to have some kind of influence from you."

I rub at my eyes and roll over, shutting off the light, shutting the room in black. Still, I can hear my parents and still I can see the definition of Joseph on the wall. I picture him leaning in close. He tucks my hair behind my ear and whispers, *You're a smart girl, Peyton. You're such a smart girl, you know that?*

Those words used to make me feel good, used to give me confidence, but with Joseph's influence, all I feel is the white heat coiling deep down inside of me.

———

STALIN HAD ONE DAUGHTER, Svetlana. There's a photo of him carrying her in my book. Svetlana's nine in the photo, but she looks far too old to be carried in his arms. It makes me wonder when she stopped calling him Daddy.

I remember being nine, the night Dad came home from his office job and said he'd been laid off. That was when they started arguing at night. Back then it was about paying the mortgage, the bills. Mom wasn't working back then, but that was when she started drifting from job to job, always quitting because she didn't like something about the work she had to do, always starting another job because she had no other choice.

The weekend trips to the bookstore ended. Even discount books were too expensive. Dad took me to the library on the weekends he didn't have to work. We'd ride our bikes there. He'd lock my bike beside his on the rack outside, even though I had my own lock, even though I was perfectly capable of doing it myself.

When he got his job at the drive-thru oil change, he started to look tired, so tired, always worn out, with these dark lines on his face he'd try to wash off.

Those lines just got deeper and more defined the older I got.

———

ZOEY TRACES RIPPLES into her agenda, scribbles over the day with black stars and symbols with her pen. "I'm not going to be able to come over," she says.

"We haven't done much work yet," I say, trying to feign Mom's tone with my voice.

"I know," she says. "I want to. Really. I just, I can't get her to believe what I tell her. She always thinks that I'm going to go to some guy's house or something like that. She doesn't take my word for anything."

"I guess it's different for me," I say. "My mom complains to my dad about things, mostly."

"Doesn't your dad stand up for you?"

I look up.

"Isn't that what Dads are supposed to do?"

"Not really," I say.

Zoey looks down at her agenda, tightening her grasp around her pen, the tip threatening to blacken the entire page. "I never met my real Dad," she says. "My step-dad's an asshole, so it's not like I really ever talk to him about anything." She shrugs before looking up at me. "It's just a weird thought I have sometimes. Sometimes I wonder what it'd be like having a guy around that I can like, you know, talk to about things."

"It's not that big of a deal," I say. "It was better when I was a kid, when we'd go out and get books and stuff."

"Why don't you just ask him to take you again?"

"I don't know," I say. "It's just different." I hesitate, trying to come up with a reason, thinking of being a kid and sitting on Dad's lap. The thought just makes my skin crawl now. I think back to when Dad first told me all about Stalin. He showed me all Joseph's photos and I told him that I thought Stalin looked kind of nice. Then Dad told me the truth.

"We don't have a lot in common," I say.

She gives me her printed paragraphs of exposition. They're sloppily-written, but Zoey's got such a worn look on her face. She makes me feel tired, makes me feel weak, defeated. I show her all of the photos I've scanned from my books. I show her all the photos of Stalin, from youth to General Secretary. She picks up the picture of Stalin carrying Svetlana and she studies it for a few seconds before saying anything.

"This is his daughter, right?" she asks.

I nod.

She looks back at the photo and smirks. "It's weird to think he was a dad."

"Yeah," I say, taking the picture back, studying Svetlana's gaze. She looks like she's telling me something, looks like she wants me to stop.

———

I copy text from the books, reciting things I've learned. I can't ignore the obvious things, like how I'm not even really paraphrasing but plagiarizing. Mr. Allen will notice when I cite my sources, so I tell myself to return and rewrite it all later because I'm bored and tired and done, and when I press my face into my hands all I can feel are the creases in my forehead.

Dad walks past my bedroom. He pokes his head in the door and my heart starts to pound.

"How's your project coming along?" he asks.

"Fine," I say.

"Good." He smiles a middle-aged Joseph Stalin smile and continues down the hall.

I try to rewrite Zoey's exposition while the shower whirs in the bathroom, the white noise a distraction. I stare at the photos, black and white and fuzzy. I stare at Stalin, still feeling the static between my legs, feeling the static in my chest, reverberations trickling between my ribs, tickling me inside.

There's a knock on the door and I look up and glance at Dad's face, cleaned and expressionless. He stands in the frame, doesn't take a step into the room, hands buried in the pockets of his jeans. He glances at the wall. Stalin's gone but his influence isn't.

"You coming down for dinner?" Dad asks.

"In a minute," I say.

He doesn't wait. He shuts the door when he leaves.

———

Zoey finally comes to help. She brings a red sheet of poster board and a pad of construction paper. I finish my write-ups on Stalin, struggling to add extra information on his tyrannical middle-aged existence. I print them out but she doesn't read them over. She doesn't seem to notice how short my paragraphs are. She doesn't pay attention to the large font. She cuts them out, keen with her scissors.

I start printing out new pages, large bold quotes to keep as a distraction, to use as filler.

"One death is a tragedy, the death of millions is statistic," Zoey says, smiling. "I love this quote so much." The scissors make metallic scratches in my ears, white noise that makes me think about getting clean.

"It used to scare me," I say.

She hands me the quote. "Why the hell would it scare you?" she asks.

"I don't know. It was the way my dad used to read it, I guess."

She picks up the young Stalin photo and admires it before cutting it out. She works slowly, lets the blades sear the white edges from the picture.

"I'd so do him," she fawns. "It'd be nice if there were more pictures of him in his twenties. I mean, if I could, I'd make the whole project about him in his twenties because he robbed banks and did a bunch of other badass stuff."

"Yeah," I say, redirecting my attention to the footsteps in the hall.

"I mean, seriously," she says, flipping the photo so I can look at it. "Wouldn't you let him do all sorts of stuff to you?"

My mouth opens and my heated exhale dries the saliva on my tongue.

She positions the photo in the centre of the poster, making it the real focal point, his face overpowering all the haunting quotes, all the truths Dad told me.

"It's kind of plain-looking," Zoey says.

"It's because we didn't do enough research," I say, my breath heavy.

"Well, what do we do?" she asks. "I thought you said we were totally going to get an A on this."

"I did as much as I could," I say. "I've researched this to death and I've done like, practically all of the work."

"What?" Zoey asks.

I look at her and hesitate. "This just, this always happens," I say. "I do all this work on a project where I'm supposed to be working with other people. It's exhausting."

She drops the scissors. "It's not my fault I haven't been able to come over," she says. "My mom's been such a raging bitch all week. She wouldn't let me out. I really tried, okay?" She withdraws, sitting back, pulling her agenda into her lap.

"Well," I say. "I don't know; we could try decorating it. I mean, you draw all the time. You could draw something."

Zoey's expression changes. She leans forward and tears off a piece of red paper. "We could do some cut-outs, different symbols and stuff, like that hammer, or the curved blade thing Stalin used."

"It's a sickle," I say.

"Whatever," she says. "I just don't want to fail, okay? My mom will freak if I fail another class."

———

AT NIGHT, Mom and Dad don't argue. I can hear them talking through the wall and I cup my hand over my ear, straining to hear their conversation.

For the first time their voices are too quiet to understand, hushed white noise from the other room.

———

WE GET A C.

The poster gets hung in the hallway, but Mr. Allen's note on the board is too much to leave exposed: *Nice artistic effort, but you seem to have focused more on Stalin's early years than on his significance in WWII.*

Dad picks me up from school. I toss the poster in the back seat, but he turns his head to glance at bold red grade. The apple bobs hard in his throat. His fingers tense around the gear shift as he puts the car in drive.

"I thought you would have done better," he says.

"I know," I say, buckling myself in. "I never do all that well with group projects."

"You were distracted," he says, putting the car into gear.

I swallow, feeling my grasp tighten around my seatbelt, adjusting it over the pounding in my chest. Breathing in, all I can smell is oil and grime.

"You don't get C's, Peyton," he says, eyes on the road, staring with such intensity it's like he's not even looking at anything at all. His fingers turn white, grasping the wheel. "I taught you to know better. You're a smart girl, Peyton."

"Dad, I tried."

"You're a smart girl," he says again, his voice raised.

"It's not my fault!" I burst. "Zoey barely helped at all. She made me do all the research..."

"I taught you all about Joseph Stalin!"

The light ahead changes; he steps on the brake, tires screeching. The seat belt digs into my chest, preventing me from lurching forward as the car halts over the line. I'm held back against my seat, unable to breathe.

Dad grabs for my wrist but I snatch it away, still finding myself caught in his stare.

"He was a terrible man, Peyton. Joseph Stalin was a terrible man."

It's hard to breathe, the air snatched out of me. My lip twitches, muscles forcing a frown. Blinking, I push my head back against the headrest, letting my gaze stray to the green light. Dad continues to stare, his influence infecting my lungs with a burning ache, making me feel like I've been holding my breath forever.

Cars behind us start honking.

Dad swallows. He shakes his head and adjusts his grasp over the wheel before he turns his focus back to the road.

"I should have expected it," he says. His voice sounds tight in his throat. "You had to grow up eventually," he says.

I lean my head against the window and my fingers tighten around the door handle. I wish I could just open it and jump out.

———

THEY ARGUE AGAIN, only this time it's Dad's voice that's backed with emotion.

I send a text to Zoey, my fingers shaking when I tell her that my parents are fighting, that they're talking about me.

She responds within the minute, her text reading, *omg, that sucks.* Then she sends another that reads, *keep calm and think about stalin,* followed by another text that reads, *LOL!*

I set my phone down but then it vibrates again, another message from Zoey that reads, *btw, my mom was totally stoked about the C!*

———

I TEAR DOWN JOSEPH after school the next day. I take down Earnest and Wilfred and Johannes. I crumple up Nathan and Leon. I pull Lewis off the wall and toss him with the rest into the trash. Behind each picture is a pristine patch of lilac paint, a slightly darker shade than the one I thought my walls were all this time.

I don't do my homework.

Lying back, I stare at the vacant wall with no fantasies. I lay there until my Dad knocks on the door. He pauses when he notices the emptiness behind me.

"Dinner's ready," he says. He doesn't wait for me. He turns and goes downstairs.

———

ZOEY SITS BESIDE ME in class. She taps her anarchy pen on the desk. "Look," she says, "I know you, like, did most of the work, but I'd totally try to help more if you want to be my partner for the next project."

"I don't know," I say.

"Hey, look," she says. She opens her agenda and she shows me the Stalin picture that she's taped inside. She's drawn a heart around his face. "Cool, hey?"

I look at Joseph. Heat fills me again. All the terrible things Dad told me about Joseph don't matter. It's the look on Joseph's face that matters. It's full of lust. It's full of desire. It's all I can do to look away.

YOU THOUGHT ABOUT BUYING HER AN ICE PACK OR MAYBE FLOWERS.

PLOT POINTS

DENOUEMENT:

Your new apartment has hardwood floors and brown walls. You can't help but think it looks like the inside of a coffin.

What really sold you was the kitchen. The layout was functional.

You move the table by the door, put your keys in the bowl. You turn the deadbolt, but it's not like you ever have to worry about her stumbling in. You're supposed to be able to breathe now, but you can't.

Behind you is all your past life bullshit crammed into cardboard boxes.

You'll have to unpack it all eventually.

RESOLUTION:

She was the one who filed for divorce.

She came out of the bedroom in her dark makeup and her short black dress. She slid the papers in front of you and said, "Just sign them. I don't care."

You couldn't find a pen. You looked everywhere. You tore through all the drawers and you left them all open. The kitchen always looked like shit anyway.

You made a drink instead. You ended up playing with two magnets you picked off the fridge. You pried them apart and put them together. You tried to touch the same poles together but all you felt was the pressure working between your hands. You kept trying to connect the magnets, but the weight built in your chest, climbed up the back of your throat and behind your eyes.

You remembered you still had a pen in your shirt pocket and you finally shed the burden.

You finally gave up.

FALLING ACTION—2:

She confessed a lot of things the night she took all those pills.

She said, "I've fucked plenty of guys."

She said, "I'm not even attracted to you anymore."

She said, "Sometimes I feel like the only way to get away from you is to kill myself."

You wanted to leave but you forced her to drink the ipecac. She'd forever be a tangle of mania and depression. You just wanted to be a good husband, so you held your breath and tried to deal.

FALLING ACTION—1:

She refused to look at you. She kept the bedroom door locked. You didn't want to break it open. There were so many dents from all the times you'd hit it before. You pressed your ear to the door and heard nothing. For a moment you wondered if she'd gone through with it.

You said, "Liz?"

She said, "Fuck you, Trevor."

You thought about buying her an ice pack or maybe flowers. Your entire body was sore with heat and anxiety. It made you wonder if that was what she felt like all the time.

Your knuckles ached, and you wondered how long they would.

CLIMAX:

The blood on her face matched her shirt.

She'd sucked all your patience, always coming home late at night. You didn't really care who she'd been with, but you were tired and angry and you needed something to blame her for. You called her a cunt, a bitch, a whore.

You said, "It's the truth. It's the fucking truth."

She pulled the glasses out of the cupboards. There wasn't much left to break in the kitchen but she always found something to throw at you. She was always angrier than you.

You couldn't breathe anymore.

You made a fist.

RISING ACTION—3:

You probably should have forced her to see a doctor. You read stories on the Internet about other couples with demolished homes. Somehow they managed to limit the damage. You knew you'd never have that dream kitchen you both wanted. All you really cared about was a kitchen that didn't have dents on all the cabinet doors.

Renovations were a lot of work, though.

You were exhausted enough already.

RISING ACTION—2:

She missed too much work and she lost her job. She cried and apologized. She said she'd get herself together and find a new job, but you told her to give herself a break.

You said, "It's okay."

She fit perfectly in your arms, her warmth soothing your chest. She was easier to deal with when her face was white and her eyes were puffy. She never looked for a job, though. She spent weeks cooped up in the house. The bills piled up and she started getting restless again.

You came home from work and asked, "How are you feeling today?"

She said, "Stop pestering me, Trevor."

She rolled her eyes and went to the bedroom. She put on makeup. She put on a black dress you'd never seen before. She took her purse.

You asked, "Where are you going?"

She said, "I'm so fucking tired of you."

She grew tired of things so quickly.

RISING ACTION—1:

You bought new plates. She pretended like you were filling your wedding registry, going through the aisles, smiling, looking like she did when you met her.

She picked up a plate with sky blue trim and birds on the edge.

She said, "Don't you love this?"

She loved the new plates more than the previous set, but in the back of your head you wondered how soon it would be before you had to replace them.

INCITING INCIDENT:

She wanted the house because of the kitchen. It was the first house you both looked at, but she fell in love with the granite counters and the birch cabinets and the island bar. She said, "Trevor, I can see myself here."

Three months later she agonized over Christmas. She barely slept. She spent her nights obsessing over the decorations and the dinner.

You told her, "It's just a turkey, Liz."

She didn't believe you. She'd invited her mother and everything had to be perfect. It snowed on Christmas Eve. The phone rang early next morning. Her mother didn't want to risk the drive into town.

Lizzie's shoulders sank. Her fingers tightened and threw the phone across the room. Her chest heaved and she shoved all the plates off the kitchen island. She yelled about how exhausted she was. She said, "It's ruined. It's fucking ruined."

All you did was stare.

She met your gaze and hesitated. You didn't know what to say. She started crying. She fled to the bedroom and locked the door. Her cries echoed while you surveyed the damage in the kitchen. There was a dent on one of the cabinets where she'd thrown the phone.

EXPOSITION:

One of the service clerks came into your office and told you there was a woman sampling strawberries in the produce aisle. She wasn't who you expected, a pretty blonde with a softened gaze. Her lips were a gentle shade of pink.

You asked, "Are you alright?"

She said, "No." She put the box of strawberries down and tried to leave.

You grabbed the box and went after her. You said, "You really should buy them."

She asked, "Why?"

You hesitated. You said, "Because they're delicious."

She smiled then. She laughed. She bought the strawberries. You should have left her alone then. Still you felt a pressure pulling you to her. You wanted to see her smile forever.

THE TRAIN PULLS OUT
OF THE STATION AND I
BLINK, TRYING TO RID THE
STAIN OF HER RAINCOAT
FROM MY GAZE.

CAT CALLS

The girl is on the Skytrain again. Her red raincoat always pulls my gaze. She smiles through the window. Today her dark hair's tied back. Her lashes are curled and her eyes are lined in black, catty. My fingers tighten around the handle of my briefcase. I swallow before I board.

"You're wearing those pants again," she calls. "I always thought they defined your package real nice."

The other passengers look up. They look at her and then at me, at my black pressed slacks. My throat tightens. My gaze drops to the floor and I take a seat. I set my briefcase over my lap.

"Why don't you sit over here?" the girl asks.

The train starts, its moan filling my ears. It always sounds like a ghost getting off. I lean back against my seat and stare out the window as the train passes through the city and the rain. Then the bells chime and the speaker announces the next stop.

The next station is New Westminster.

The girl gets up. She's all legs under her raincoat. Her thighs are smooth and her calves are lean. Her platform heels click across the floor.

The bells chime again and the doors slide closed. The train starts. The moan continues.

"You never want to talk," the girl says.

My fingers tense and I meet her gaze. "Look, I'm married, alright?"

"That's okay," she says.

"It's not okay," I say. "You've been bothering me all week. I'm just, I'm not interested."

She puts her hand on her hip and her raincoat rides up, revealing the hem of her dress, floral fabric with blues and yellows, baby bedroom colours. She steps forward and straddles my leg. Her thighs rub against my slacks.

The next station is 22nd Street.

The girl leans forward and pushes her knee against my briefcase. The handle digs into my stomach. New passengers board the train, their eyes immediately on me.

"Maybe you should move your briefcase," she says.

I shift and draw a breath, looking up. Her eyes glisten. She bites her lip.

The next station is Edmonds.

"There's a war in your head, isn't there?" She braces her hands over my shoulders, pushes me back against my seat. "It's okay to admit it," she says. "There's a war in every man."

The train slows and I turn my head. Outside, the rain patters against the glass.

"You get off at Commercial-Broadway, right?" She massages my shoulders, her grasp tight, kneading pressure, an ache in my head.

I tighten my fingers around my briefcase.

She leans in closer, her breath hot against my ear. "You wanna get off now, don't you?"

———

AT WORK, the reception area is decorated with balloons and banners. Everybody jumps out from behind front desk and they yell, "Surprise!"

I hold my briefcase in front of me like I'm still on the train.

Everybody sings "Happy Birthday" and they give me a card filled with handwritten jokes and sentiments about being over the hill. At lunch, they serve cake in the break room. I bring a slice back to my office but I eat my sandwich instead.

Dick walks past the open door. "Are you not going to eat that?" he asks, looking at the cake on my desk.

I shake my head and he takes the plate. He slices a fork through the red velvet and talks through mouthfuls. "Leslie have plans for you tonight?"

"I don't think so. She's been so preoccupied with that house lately."

"The heritage Victorian on Fourth?"

"Yeah," I say. "She showed it to some buyers who seemed interested. She's been spending all her time working things out."

"That'd be a nice present, hey? A big commission check."

"What do you mean?"

"She must make more money than you, Jason. You can quit your job and live like a kept man."

"That's not funny," I say.

He laughs anyway, and I look over at the phone, remembering how Leslie used to sound when she called, the need that registered in her voice after the failure to conceive, the IVF treatments, the miscarriages, the debt. She used to spend every day at home in her blue bathrobe. It used to be I'd have to spend every lunch hour in my office so she could call. Her voice always shook over the line.

Just tell me everything will be okay.

I look up but Dick's already gone.

The crumbs of my sandwich fall on my lap.

———

The next station is 22nd Street.

The next station is New Westminster.

The next station is Columbia.

It's dark by the time I get off the train. On my way back to the apartment, I walk past Leslie's heritage Victorian. Her picture's on the For Sale sign. She's smiling, blonde hair curled, lips painted red, powerhouse.

My ears start to ache.

Leslie's already asleep when I get home. She's in her baby blue bathrobe, the bedsheets kicked around her feet. Her lamp's still on. It's almost like it used to be, except she's got housing contracts on the nightstand instead of the stack of pregnancy books she used to read.

I crawl beside her and kiss her forehead, her cheek. Her hair smells like lavender. I wrap my arms around her. I press my lips to her ear.

"I love you," I say.

She moans in her sleep. She nudges me with her elbow. She pushes me away.

———

I WRITE STRATA NOTICES over lunch. Dick walks in and stares at the crumbs on my ledger. "Jesus," he says. "Can't you give yourself a break? It's depressing enough just looking at you."

He drags me with him to the bar after work. He orders a round of Caesars. "If you're man enough, you don't give a shit that it's a cocktail," he says.

I stare at the glass, red thickness like clotted blood, test tube baby waste that goes down salty. Dick flags the waitress and orders us a second round. He looks her over when he orders a third, leans in too close when he orders a fourth. The taste of the Clamato juice settles in my gut.

"How's Leslie?" he asks.

"She was asleep when I got home last night."

He laughs. "You didn't even get laid on your birthday?"

"Why would I care about that?"

"Hey, before Alice and I split, birthdays were about the only time we ever had sex."

A Skytrain passes on the tracks outside the bar, its moan filling my ears.

"I don't really think about things like that. I can't."

Dick looks over.

I shake my head and blink, lightheaded. "All that shit, you know, not being able to conceive. It's kind of insulting. You just, you spend all that money to jack off into a bottle and then they just make a baby in a dish?" My throat tightens. I clear my throat. "Leslie painted the spare room blue and yellow. She always wanted a gender-neutral nursery."

Dick lifts his glass and takes a drink.

Another train passes outside, going the opposite direction. Its ghostly echo haunts like Leslie's voice when she called me at work the first time. She sounded so hollow, so dead.

Jason?

"She wasn't even herself the second time." My gaze drifts to the red mess in Dick's glass. "She called me every day when it got worse, you know. Then I got home from work and she was hunched over the counter."

Dick sets his glass down. He scratches his brow.

"Seeing her go through all that, I just, I did what I could."

"She reinvented herself," Dick says, staring down at the table, his fingers flinching. "You have to, after something like that."

"Yeah." I shake my head. "It's just, she didn't even tell me about becoming a Realtor until she got her license. She just said she was going to make the spare room her office. She painted the walls grey."

———

I SWAY ON THE PLATFORM until the train arrives. The first thing I notice is the raincoat. The girl is slouched in her seat. She tugs at the zipper, opens her coat to reveal her tight dress, her figure. I avert my gaze and slump into the nearest seat, setting my briefcase on the floor. The train starts and the briefcase tips over. I pick it up and set it on the empty seat beside me.

The girl walks up. She pushes the case aside and sits down.

"You're drunk," she says.

"So what?"

The train is nearly empty, just a handful of students with headphones in their ears. I stare at the reflection in the window of me slouched in my seat, her beside me. She crosses her legs. Her skirt rides up. She's wearing black panties. They're lace.

"What were you drinking?" she asks.

My ears throb to the pace in chest.

"Caesars," I say.

"That's not a very manly drink."

"So?"

She puts her hand on my thigh. "I like you better this way," she says. "You're a white flag."

The taste of the Caesar lingers in my throat. "What do you want?" I ask.

Her fingers tighten. "Tell me something," she says. "Tell me a secret. Drunk men always share secrets."

My gaze drifts to my briefcase. "I turned forty this week."

She draws a breath and her grasp moves from my leg to my hand. She touches the ring on my finger. "Did your wife give you birthday sex?"

"No." I pull my hand away.

"Why not?" she asks. "Married men still like pussy."

The train turns a bend, squealing on the tracks.

She leans in, her lips against my ear again, her voice a whisper. "How big is your dick?"

My head hurts too much to answer.

The next station is Columbia.

Her fingers trace along the crease Leslie ironed into my slacks. The train slows and the doors open. I reach for my briefcase.

"You're losing," she says.

"Losing what?" I ask, stumbling to a stand.

She glances at the briefcase. "You always look so miserable carrying that thing."

I stagger out of the train before the doors close. She smiles through the window. The train pulls out of the station and I blink, trying to rid the stain of her raincoat from my gaze.

———

THERE'S A STICKER on the sign in front of Leslie's heritage house, SOLD written in bold block letters. She pounces on me when I get home.

"Baby, it finally happened!" she says.

She's in black lace lingerie, but the dark overpowers her. She always looked better in baby blues. She claws at my chest, undoes the buttons on my shirt. The briefcase slips from my grasp. It hits the floor, the bang heavy in my ears.

Leslie shoves me against the wall.

You're a white flag.

"I want to celebrate," she says. Her lavender scent brings a headache.

In the bedroom, she climbs on top of me and writhes. She arches her back. She shakes the bed, moans in my ear, distorted sounds like the Skytrain.

Married men still like pussy.

My lungs ache when I inhale. My grasp tightens around her waist. She tilts her head back, braces her thighs around me. It's the way it always is now, her hands on my chest, pushing me down. She groans when she comes.

"God, baby," she says. "We never do this enough."

She makes it worse.

———

THE NEXT STATION is Patterson.

The next station is Joyce-Collingwood.

The next station is 29th Avenue.

The girl isn't on the train, but I leave my briefcase on my lap and I look out at every platform for her red raincoat, her bare legs.

The next station is Nanaimo.

The next station is Commercial-Broadway.

The train slows and I grip the nearby pole and stand, gravity pulling me. The bells chime. The doors slide open. The rustle of people. The city's busiest station, bodies and red all over.

You wanna get off now, don't you?

———

THERE'S A DENT on the side of my briefcase. It's difficult to get open. The papers are scattered inside, a mess of tenant applications, noise complaints and rental contracts. I work through all of it. I call references. I set up appointments. I answer every complaint with sympathy.

I'm a joke of a property manager, eating lunch at my desk.

———

THERE'S TAKE-OUT INDIAN FOOD on the counter when I get home.

Leslie clears her housing contracts off the table. She lays out a white tablecloth and serves tikka masala over rice. The food burns my throat. I stare at the plate, wincing against my headache, the pressure.

There's a war in your head, isn't there?

My fingers flinch around my fork. I set it down, getting sauce on the tablecloth. "So, this is stupid," I say. "There's this, well, there's this girl on the train sometimes."

Leslie looks up.

"She just, she says things to me."

"Like what?"

I shrug and shake my head. "Just how good my pants look. She asks me how big my dick is."

"Seriously?" Leslie asks.

"It's gone on all week," I say. "It's kind of degrading, really."

"Oh, come on," she says.

"Haven't men ever made cat calls at you?"

"Just ignore her, Jason."

"What do you think I've been doing?"

"She's probably just teasing you." Leslie buries her fork in the red on her plate. She slices through a piece of chicken. "Just take the compliment and move on," she says, laughing.

———

AT THE BAR, I empty the dregs from the beer pitcher into my glass.

"You know, the thing about Leslie?" I say. "She always gave terrible blow jobs."

"You two have a fight or something?" Dick asks.

A SkyTrain passes outside, moaning.

"Are you having an affair?" he asks.

"No," I say.

"Are you considering it?"

"No." I finish my beer, hesitating. "I still love her."

"Yeah, that's what I told myself at first," he says. "I spent years telling myself that, but with the kids grown up there was nothing to look forward to. I'd come home and Alice would have dinner ready. She'd ask me about work and I wouldn't even want to have a conversation with her. The girl at Subway was more interesting to talk to." He shrugs. "Things just happened. No sense in denying it. There was so much shit in my head."

"What about when Alice found out?" I ask.

"Honestly, it was really just a relief," he says, leaning back in his chair. He whistles at the waitress and holds up his empty glass. He thinks he's a real man, but he ogles the waitress's chest when he orders another Caesar.

———

THE LAST TRAIN of the night arrives. The girl's there, bare legs crossed, her raincoat undone. She's wearing her yellow and blue dress. The fabric clings to her figure.

Just take the compliment and move on.

The doors slide closed behind me. The girl looks up. She smiles and my headache starts to ease. I stumble across the car, slipping into the seat beside her. I drop my briefcase on the floor.

"What are you doing?" she asks.

"I don't know."

The train whirs to life.

"I like you drunk," she says. She touches my leg, runs her fingers along the crease I had to iron in because Leslie never has the time. "You look so good in black slacks."

She takes my hand. My fingers slip between hers.

"I like men like you," she says. "I like your business wear and tear, the tortured look on your face. I like your briefcase. You always look so miserable and it makes me so wet."

The next station is Royal Oak.

She parts her legs. Her thighs are pale and she runs her fingers up. She isn't wearing panties. The train slows and she slides her fingers into her folds.

"What's your name?" she asks.

"Jason," I say.

The train starts again, its moan echoing.

The girl pulls my hand between her open legs. "Do you wanna know what I feel like?"

Her skin's warm, soft. I slide my palm up her thigh and under her dress. She's smooth, her inside an abyss, slick lips warming my fingers. I stare out the window at the passing blur of all the shitty apartments that I control.

She leans in. Her lips brush against my ear. "How big is your dick, Jason?"

The next station is Patterson.

"It's six inches," I say.

"Is that not big enough for your wife?"

My throat tightens. "It used to be."

The train shakes as it slows. I slip against her. She smells like rainwater.

People board, their gazes falling toward her open legs. She clutches my hand before I can pull away.

"Let them look," she says. "Let them think what they want. I just want you to do this for me."

The train starts. My headache starts.

"Please," she begs. "Please."

She grinds herself against my palm. My thumb slips against her clit and she moans.

"Right there," she says. Her breaths are heavy, just like Leslie's when she used to call. She grips my hand. She's shaking.

Just tell me everything will be okay.

I rub her harder, thumbing circles, pushing down, two fingers buried inside of her and she writhes in the seat. Her moan echoes with the Skytrain. I lean over her, feeling her breath against my neck. Her grasp tightens. She digs her nails into my wrist and she fills the train with her moan.

The next station is Columbia.

The train slows and I look up. The other passengers turn their heads.

The girl exhales, her chest heaving. "You're so good," she says. Her fingers loosen and I pull my hand away.

My palm's still wet, smelling of her.

I bury my hand in my pocket, leaving the briefcase behind.

———

THE SUN STREAMS IN through the curtains and I roll out of bed with a new headache, the girl's voice in my head.

How big is your dick, Jason?

Leslie's in the bathroom, standing before the mirror in her baby blue robe, her blonde hair tied back.

"Jason?"

I stumble into the hallway and she turns and meets my gaze. Her eyes are bright, glistened with tears. She's holding a pregnancy test and there are two red lines in the oval window.

"Can you read this?" she asks. "I need you to read this." She gives me the test and the box, even though I don't need it to tell me what the two lines mean.

I rub at the stubble on my face. My fingers still smell like pussy.

HE WAS THE ONLY
ONE WAVING
GOODBYE.

MODERN BEASTS

The library had never looked like the sort of building that welcomed visitors. Its bare cement walls towered above Eva when her mother pulled her car up front. The big glass doors reflected silver in her eyes, looking like the doorway of a fortress compared to all of the nearby shops with their banners, flowers and sidewalk umbrellas.

Eva's mother leaned over and gave Eva a cold kiss on the cheek. "This place is just a daycare the government pays for," she said. "It's a public building and you have every right to be here, Eva. You have to remember to tell them that, okay?"

Eva nodded, her fingers tightening around the straps of her floral backpack.

"You have to be strong," Eva's mother said. "Make your voice heard."

"Okay," Eva said. She stepped out of the car. She wished she could have gone with her mother to wave the big signs she'd helped colour the night before, but her mother shut the door and drove off, already with an angry look on her face.

Eva walked into the dense wilderness of books, her body tense when she spotted Mindy, the head librarian. Mindy's face was always ghostly pale—her thin red lips pressed tightly together. Mindy walked up, her long black cardigan billowing behind her like a cape.

"Is your mom grocery shopping again?" Mindy asked.

"She's protesting today," Eva said.

"Where?" Mindy asked.

"I don't remember," Eva said. "A man's office. Mommy says he works for the government."

"You know that I technically work for the government," Mindy said.

Eva tensed. She swallowed. "My mommy said I have rights. She said that I'm allowed to be here."

Mindy tucked her hair behind her ear and crouched down so her face was close to Eva's. Her eyes always looked so dark because her mascara was constantly smeared. "Your mommy isn't right about everything, Eva. She can't just leave you here."

Eva lifted her backpack. "My mommy gave me snacks so I'll be okay."

Mindy pointed at the sign above her desk with a picture of pop and chips with a line struck through. "You can't eat in here," she said. "And you're not old enough to be here by yourself."

Eva took a step back and tightened her fists. She wanted to tell Mindy how hungry she was. She wanted to be the strong seven-year-old girl her mother always said she was, but she couldn't mirror the anger in Mindy's stare.

The front doors opened and a warm brush of air swept through the library. A man walked in carrying a cup of coffee and a newspaper from the cafe across the street. He made eye contact with Mindy and smiled. He had wavy brown hair and a beard—burly shoulders straining against a plaid flannel shirt.

"I thought you could use a coffee," the man said. He handed Mindy the cup and kissed her on the lips. Mindy took the coffee. She looked happy for a moment, but her smile faded when she looked down at Eva again. The man placed his hand on Mindy's shoulder and asked what was wrong.

"It's Eva," Mindy said, her voice deepening. "Her mother's some kind of activist. She leaves her here all the time so she can protest whatever it is she's angry about."

The man looked down at Eva and smiled. "I don't mind watching her," he said.

"Could you?" she asked. "You've always been better with kids."

"It's no problem," he said, kneeling down. He extended his hand to Eva, his fingers wrapping gently around her palm. "It's nice to meet you, Eva. My name is Owen and I'm a friend of Mindy's. Would you like to read with me?"

"Yes," Eva said, "but I'm hungry. I brought a snack but I'm not allowed to eat it."

Owen looked up at Mindy.

"You can take her to the break room if you want," Mindy said. "I'll feel a lot better if I know she's with you instead of by herself."

"How about that, Eva?" Owen asked. "You can eat your snack and then I can read you a story. I'm sure that together we can find a good book to read." He took her hand and tucked the newspaper under his arm. "The paper never has good news anyway."

"That's what my mom always says," Eva echoed, her fingers loosening from the straps of her backpack.

The room Mindy led them to had grey walls and a dull floor with peeling square tiles. A table sat in the centre, its surface dulled and faded. Eva rubbed her hand over the surface but the dirt didn't come off. She caught Mindy staring at her and she leaned close to Owen because his shirt was red and warm.

"I'll make sure she's safe," Owen promised. Mindy nodded and turned, leaving Eva alone with Owen.

Eva shared her oatmeal cookies with Owen. She laughed when the crumbs got stuck in his beard. Owen said that he used to give tours at the museum, but over the years he'd developed arthritis in his knees and it hurt too much to walk around all day.

"Do you give tours of the library now?" Eva asked.

"No," Owen said. "I just like to spend my days here. I get to read and I get to see Mindy. She doesn't let me eat in the library, either, but sometimes we go out for dinner."

Eva looked out the break room door. Mindy sat at her desk in her big swivel chair, her back turned and her shoulders strained. She ate her salad while she worked, piercing the lettuce with a silver fork. Her dark hair was coiled tight into a bun. Her exposed neck was pale and long, reminding Eva of the pretty swans at the park that swam away from her when she tried to feed them.

The air vent whirred to life and the break room grew cold. Eva started to shiver, but then Owen leaned in.

"Do you like fairy tales, Eva?" he asked.

Eva nodded, and Owen brought her to the bright children's section of the library. Trees were painted on the walls and the sun shone through the windows. The shelves brimmed with stories that Owen and Eva searched through. Eva showed Owen a book called Bluebeard. Owen took the book and shook his head.

"I don't think you'll like this one, Eva."

"Why not?" Eva asked.

"Because this story doesn't have a happy ending."

"I thought all fairy tales were supposed to have happy endings," Eva said.

"Some fairy tales are supposed to teach you lessons," Owen said.

"I don't like those kinds of stories," Eva said. "I want a story with a happy ending."

Owen agreed, and so he helped Eva pick out a stack of better books. He read her *The Little Mermaid* and *Sleeping Beauty*, but Eva's favourite story was the tale of *Snow White* and the seven men who protected her from the evil queen.

Owen's voice warmed Eva's chest, but then Eva heard her mother's voice calling. Eva got up from her seat. She picked up her backpack and started toward her mother, but then Mindy stood, her rushed footsteps heavy over the floor.

Eva froze, her heart pounding.

"I ought to call the police on you," Mindy said, walking right up to Eva's mother, pointing in her face. "You have no idea who your daughter's with or what she's doing while she's here."

Eva's mother bit her lip, standing tall. "My daughter is a smart young girl," she said. "She knows how to look out for herself. You make her sound completely helpless."

"She's a little girl!" Mindy said. "She can't protect herself from everything."

"Do you have kids?" Eva's mother asked.

Mindy hesitated.

"Well, then you have no right to judge me," she said. "Why does my daughter's safety fall solely in my hands? Isn't everyone responsible for a child's well being? What if you noticed she was in trouble? Wouldn't you do something about it?"

"I noticed that your little girl could get into all kinds of trouble without her parent, and I'm trying to do something about it now."

Eva's mother laughed. "All this community does is judge single parents like me."

"I swear to God I'll call the police the next time she's here by herself," Mindy said.

"It's so typical, how everyone's response is to blame the parent."

"Exactly," Mindy said. "You're her parent. You'd never forgive yourself if something happened to her."

"And you wouldn't forgive yourself, either, because it's obvious that you know what's really at issue here. There's no support in this society. I'm a parent and I have to do what I have to do. All you're doing is blaming the victim."

"She's the victim!" Mindy shouted, pointing her red finger at Eva. "She's the real victim, and I swear to you I will call the police the next time I see her in here alone."

Everybody in the library stared at Eva. She could hardly breathe when everything was all her fault. The tears burned her eyes, but Owen pulled her hands away from her face.

"It's going to be okay," he said, his voice gentle in her ear. "Just go and tell your mother you want to go home." He guided Eva out of her chair and eased her forward.

Eva clutched her backpack against her chest, trying to warm the hollow ache that filled her. She pulled her mother's sleeve but all her mother did was mirror Mindy's stare.

"C'mon, Eva," she said. "It's time to go."

Eva looked back at Owen. He was the only one waving goodbye.

———

MINDY DIDN'T CALL the police the next time Eva walked into the library alone. Eva noticed the coffee on Mindy's desk, and so she wandered through the stacks until she found Owen sitting at the table in the back corner of the library. He smiled at her and patted the stack of books he'd already chosen to read to her. He pulled her onto his lap and wrapped his big arm over her shoulders. His flannel shirt warmed her skin.

Owen read about Little Red Riding Hood's journey through the woods. Eva pointed to the picture of the woodsman who rescued Red at the end of the book.

"He looks like you," she said.

"He does, doesn't he?" Owen asked.

Eva looked at the picture of Red, studying her dark hair. Eva wished that she had dark hair. She looked up to tell Owen, but then she noticed Mindy approaching the table. Mindy's eyes were friendly and warm and she smiled at Owen, but then her gaze changed when she connected with Eva.

"Where is your mother today, Eva?" Mindy asked. She leaned in close, her breath smelling like the wintergreen mints that Eva's mother always sucked in the car.

"She's at her meeting," Eva said, leaning back against the hard seat.

"What meeting?" Mindy asked. "How important must this meeting be that she leaves you here?"

Eva remembered all the things her mother had told her to say, about how it took a village to raise a child, about how the community didn't care.

"Owen likes me," Eva said. "He cares."

Eva studied Mindy's face. Her smeared mascara made her eyes look like shadows.

"Owen's not your guardian, Eva."

Eva looked at Owen. He sank back against his seat and Mindy stood over them, her lips tightening, her dark eyes turning into slits like a sinister queen plotting in front of a faded mirror.

"Honestly, Eva, I think you're better off waiting for your mother in the break room," she said. "Maybe I can read you a book when I'm on my break. How does that sound?" She reached out for Eva's hand, her red pointy nails digging into Eva's skin.

Eva struggled. She didn't want to go back to the cold grey room again.

"I want to stay with Owen," Eva said, wrestling away from Mindy's grasp. She climbed back onto Owen's lap and wrapped her arms around him. He patted her back. He told her she would be okay.

"Why didn't you tell me she was here?" Mindy asked Owen.

"You have work to do," Owen said. "I was only trying to help."

"I don't think we're helping her if we let her come here without any consequences."

"It's not Eva's fault. We'll talk to her mother, I promise you."

Mindy blinked and looked up at the ceiling. She rubbed her forehead and drew a breath.

"Everything's fine," Owen said. "I'll find you when her mother shows up, okay?"

Mindy nodded before glancing at Eva again. Her expression looked like the angry faces of the people in the newspaper Eva's mother always ranted about. Mindy sighed and walked back to her desk, wringing her hands the entire way.

"My mommy's always mad," Eva said. "She says she's mad at the government. She always writes letters on her computer. She says she can't find a job that pays enough money but nobody ever writes her back."

"Do you know what the government is?" Owen asked.

"It's the big castle," Eva said. "It has a flag. Mommy says that the people who live there don't want to help her."

"That's too bad," Owen said. "Maybe if we went to the castle we could tell all the people there not to argue. Maybe then they would listen."

"I don't want Mommy and Mindy to argue," Eva said.

Owen leaned in, his voice a whisper in Eva's ear. "When your mother arrives, I promise I'll help you get to her without without Mindy noticing."

"You promised Mindy you would tell her," Eva asked.

"Sometimes people can't keep all of their promises," Owen said, smiling.

Eva smiled back at him. She didn't care so much that her hair wasn't dark like Red's.

"You can't tell anyone that I helped you," Owen said. "It would make Mindy mad."

"I won't tell," Eva said.

"This is our little secret, okay?"

"Okay," Eva said.

Then Owen showed her the new book he'd picked out: the story of Cinderella. Eva had heard about Cinderella many times before, so she sat beside him, waiting patiently for the part where the prince would save her from the evil women.

———

OWEN READ *BEAUTY AND THE BEAST* the next week. Eva sat on Owen's lap but she kept looking over at Mindy's desk. Mindy looked different, her expression lost as she shifted her attention between her computer screen and the printer. She took a quick sip of her coffee. Her fingers shifted over her mouse, furiously clicking until the printer whirred to life. Mindy looked up, her eyes widening when she met Eva's gaze.

Eva looked up to tell Owen, but then he reached the part of the story where Beauty kissed the Beast and broke the spell on the castle.

"This is the best part, isn't it?" Owen asked, putting his arm around Eva's waist. He squeezed her torso, his grasp tight around her bony frame.

Mindy walked up to the table before Owen could turn to the page where the Beast transformed into the handsome prince he really was.

"Owen," Mindy said. Her chin shook and she struggled to gain her breath. She clutched several crumpled pages from the printer in her hand. "Can you come with me, Owen?"

"I'm in the middle of this story," he said.

"No," she said. "Put her down."

"What?" Owen asked.

"Put her down," Mindy said, her teeth gritting. "Don't make me do this in front of her."

"What you talking about?" Owen asked.

Mindy's fingers shook over the pages and she slapped them down on the table.

Owen's picture was on the first page, but it didn't really look like Owen. In the picture, Owen didn't have a beard and his hair was longer, greasier. He had stubble that looked like dirt on his jawline. He wasn't smiling. There were big bold words on the bottom of the page.

"What's that say?" Eva asked, but Owen didn't read the words aloud. His grasp loosened around her side.

"I found this on Family Watchdog," Mindy said, her lips twitching. "I already called the police."

Owen closed the book and put the picture down.

"You used to give children tours at the museum," Mindy said. Her fingers twitched and her eyes turned glossy and red. "You said you had to leave the museum because of your knee." She brought her shaking hand to her mouth and blinked.

Eva pulled at Owen's shirt.

"Get away from her," Mindy said, her voice raised. "Put her down, Owen. Put her down now."

People looked up, but they didn't look at Eva this time. This time they all looked at Owen.

"I have to go," he said, pushing Eva off his lap. He stood up and started walking for the door. "I'm sorry, Eva, but you probably won't see me again."

"Why?"

Owen didn't answer. Eva went to chase after him, but Mindy grabbed Eva's arm.

"You can't go with him," Mindy said, her wavering voice desperate in Eva's ear.

Eva kicked and thrashed against Mindy's grasp. She screamed Owen's name but Owen didn't look back.

Mindy dug her nails deep and pulled Eva back to the table. She gripped her fingers over Eva's tiny shoulders and forced her to sit in the cold hard seat. She stared at Eva with her sick red eyes, her coffee breath touching Eva's face. "You can't go with him, Eva. Owen is a bad man."

Sirens sounded outside.

"He's not the man he said he was, Eva."

Eva struggled, her eyes looking at the picture of Owen on the table. He looked like the beast that everybody in the community wanted dead.

"You're safe," Mindy said, her cold grasp locking Eva to the chair. "I promise you'll be safe," Mindy said. Her mascara was smeared and her tears ran black down her face.

Eva couldn't look at Mindy. Everybody else in the library was staring, their hushed whispers echoing between the dense towers of books. Her eyes burned as she struggled, and she spotted the cover of *Bluebeard* on the shelf behind Mindy. The man on the cover had a beard like Owen's, but his stare matched those of everyone else in the library. They all stood around her, their eyes like tiny flickering fireflies in a dark expanding forest.

SHE THINKS ABOUT HOW
ALL BOUQUETS ARE
REALLY JUST DETACHED
FLOWERS IN THE
PROCESS OF DYING.

GHOST STORY

Melody rolls over in the morning and reaches toward Lewis' side of the bed, clutching only a handful of the hotel's white sheets, luxury thousand thread count slipping smooth under her palm. She calls her boyfriend's name but there's no answer.

Propping herself up, she glances out the second-floor window at London's dreary dawn, unable to see the appeal. She'd never been much of a traveller. Lewis had gone on several vacations but this was their first trip abroad in the four years they'd been together. Melody was nervous on the plane, sitting tense with her grasp braced over the armrest. Lewis held her hand during the take-off. He whispered in her ear, promising that the dread brimming inside her would subside once they'd arrived.

Now Melody breathes over the hotel window and traces his name onto the cold glass. She glances at the London sidewalk until the condensation thickens and beads. Droplets of water slip down the pane, pulling Lewis' name into the low-hanging clouds of morning.

———

HE DOESN'T COME BACK.

Melody calls his phone and it vibrates on the nightstand beside her. She picks it up, clutching the cold plastic as she circles the room.

Lewis' jacket hangs in the closet. His clothes wait folded inside his suitcase, still seated on the luggage stand positioned at the foot of the bed. His shoes lay tossed beside the door where he kicked them off the night before.

Melody bends down and picks up the shoes, the flimsy canvas fabric still damp from the rain. She sets them together beside the door, positioned back against the wall next to her own rain-soaked flats.

"I really don't want to go," echoes a British voice in the hall.

Melody listens, drawn to the soft feminine accent from outside. The polite British tone is a change from the condescending upward whine of the girls at home. She leans against the door and glances out the peephole, its mutated circle view revealing the two maids in the hallway, a brunette and a redhead waiting for the elevator to arrive.

"Your hands are shaking," the redhead says.

"I tend to avoid the third floor," the brunette says. "Especially this time of year. October's when most of the activity occurs. I don't like to mention it. There's no sense in scaring the guests who don't know."

"About Room 333?" the redhead asks, her voice lowered to a hush.

"I believe in all those things," the brunette says.

The elevator opens and the brunette pushes the linen cart into the waiting car, its wheels squeaking. The doors ease closed again and Melody watches the empty hallway until the light above the elevator counts up to the next floor.

Morning fades. Rain continues to fall. The elevator doors open and close over the course of the day; taking passengers and exchanging them with new guests. Lewis is never one of the people to return.

Melody lies on the bed, soft sheets draped over her body. She's motionless, tense—unable to move. Creaks sound from above and she glances at the ceiling. She clenches her fists, reminding herself that she's in room 233. Her gaze traces the creak of the footsteps and she realizes which room is above.

She wonders what sort of activity the brunette was so afraid of.

———

EVENING ARRIVES. Their reservation time at the five-star restaurant down the street passes.

Melody takes the elevator to the hotel lobby and explains to the receptionist that her boyfriend's gone missing.

"His name is Lewis Peterson," she says. "I haven't seen him all day. He never told me he was going anywhere. He hasn't tried to call. I haven't heard anything."

The receptionist nods. She's a pretty blonde with the name "Pippa" printed on the tag on her chest. Pippa says she's sorry, that she hasn't seen Lewis, though her accent makes it seem almost like she isn't actually sorry at all, making the entire conversation feel like a scene in one of those British cringe comedies that Lewis always forced Melody to watch. He'd sit beside her unable to control his laughter but Melody could never understand what was so hilarious about awkward misunderstanding.

Now she laughs because she doesn't know what else to do.

Pippa looks at her and cringes.

"I'm sorry," Melody says.

This is where the comedy would cut to a commercial break, except British television doesn't really have commercials. Pippa stares and time keeps going; British time that makes Melody feel like she's eight hours ahead of herself.

———

MELODY CALLS HER SISTER, but her sister was never a big fan of Lewis.

"I hate to say it," her sister says, "but he probably left you. He's probably been talking to some British chick all this time. He probably set up this whole vacation just so he could meet her."

Melody shakes her head, the sobs burning up her throat. "All his stuff is here," she says. "He didn't take anything with him."

"Why would he need it?" her sister asks.

"He wouldn't just leave," Melody insists. "Lewis would never do something so cruel." She speaks with authority, her voice quickly tainted with whine as she thinks about all the times she and Lewis would argue and he'd storm off and slam the door, only to return with flowers and a sorry expression. The flowers always came with a card with his written sentiment:

You're a Melody.

Evidence.

Facts.

Proof.

Her sister's sigh sounds like ghostly static over the line. "I know it hurts, Melody, but what else could have happened? You can't deny that it's the only logical explanation."

Love isn't based on logic, Melody thinks. Then another set of creaks sound from the room over her head and she glances up, her fingers gripping the phone.

———

THE NEXT MORNING she goes back down to the lobby. Pippa's there, smiling her polite British smile. Melody can't help but feel anger when she remembers her sister's words from the night before.

Some British chick.

Pippa says that Lewis never appeared on the lobby's security footage.

"Okay." Melody swallows, shifting on shaking legs. She braces her hands over the desk and forces herself to meet Pippa's pale-faced expression of ambivalence. She wants to ask if she can watch the entire tape of dead night footage, but she knows how stupid and unstable she'd look if she said it aloud.

Her cold palms slip from the desk as she backs away. Her fingers curl into fists as she paces unsteady over the lobby's marble floor, back to the elevator. She rides inside the car, picturing Lewis wandering the hotel halls without his shoes. She thinks of him knocking on a closed door that isn't theirs and a chill slips over her. The feeling buries deep inside her stomach, creating an ache that cripples like plane turbulence.

She returns to the hotel room and brews a coffee from the machine. It doesn't taste right. It's muddy on her tongue, tainted somehow. The mug says *I Love London*, except the word *love* is a picture of a red heart. She thinks how stupid it is that the little heart is supposed to mean love when it looks nothing like the pounding organ in her chest.

———

THEY WERE SUPPOSED TO RIDE the London Eye on their third day. This is what she tells the police officer in his blue uniform. He doesn't look at her, just scribbles her rambling down in his tiny notebook. He nods and asks, "When was the last time you saw Lewis?"

She thinks about the sex they had the night of their arrival, how even in a different bed their lovemaking was exactly the same. She lay underneath him pretending to enjoy his attention until he came and rolled beside her, saying, "I Love You" without any real enthusiasm.

Melody laughs, remembering now that she fell asleep while he was still on top of her. She wonders if he even said he loved her at all.

"Excuse me?" the officer asks. "Ma'am?"

"We were fucking," she says.

The officer makes a face and then writes in the notebook. He tells her that he'll call if any new information arises. After he leaves, Melody lies in the middle of the bed, her arms stretched out across its width. Instead of Lewis' face it's just the ceiling over her. She stares at the intricate details of the moulding around the light, focusing on the creaking footsteps of the guests in the room above.

———

AT NIGHT she opens the mini bar and she takes out a bottle of cream liquor, drinking it back with another cup of coffee from the machine. She looks at herself in the bathroom mirror, repeating the vulgar word she said to the officer.

"Fucking."

The word sounds blunt in her American accent.

The coffee's stale but the liquor brings back some of the taste. She chugs its lukewarm comfort in large gulps, thinking of all the times Lewis came home with take-out dinner and a bouquet of flowers. He'd always set the flowers down on the table and tell her how much he really loved her, how sorry he was that he always took her for granted.

You're a Melody.

She thinks about all the bouquets she received over the course of the last four years, all the pretty arrangements that yellowed and withered and died on that dining room table. She thinks about how all bouquets are really just detached flowers in the process of dying.

"Fucking. Fucking. Fucking."

She knows how bad it sounds. She knows how much time she's wasted.

"Fucking *idiot*," she says. "You're a *fucking* idiot."

THE FLOOR CREAKS above her over the course of the night. Melody leaves the room and wanders down the hallways with the *I Love London* mug clutched in her grasp, the ceramic marked with dried remains of stale coffee. She holds the mug up to random doors, listening, thinking of what she'd hear if Lewis was behind one of them with another woman.

Love is only an emotion, and emotions are only signals sent from the brain, signals telling her body what to feel and how to react.

What she feels now is gut instinct.

The idea that Lewis' disappearance is unexplainable makes her heart pound in her chest. The idea that he'll never come back fills her body with adrenaline, and she wanders the entire span of the hotel's second-floor hallway, holding her mug up to every door, searching for evidence that the hotel is haunted, proof that her suspicions are real.

She isn't stupid anymore.

She boards the elevator and presses the button to investigate the third floor. The doors close in front of her. The lights in the car flicker. Her fingers flinch over the mug and she stands frozen, waiting, but all she hears is the ghostly moan of the car starting.

The elevator creaks and shudders before landing on the third floor. The doors rustle open. Cold air filters in, prickling her flesh like the London air she hasn't felt since she arrived in the hotel. She peeks out the elevator, glancing at the sealed door of the room directly above hers.

Room 333.

She doesn't get out.

——

MELODY'S SISTER used to say that starting over wouldn't be so bad.

The hotel is full of ghosts, different spirits in transition. This is what Melody learns, eating room service breakfast in bed with a computer on her lap. There's a ghost with a gaping wound in his face that wanders the hotel's hallways. There's the ghost of a German prince that spends his days walking through closed doors. There's a ghost known for tipping guests out of bed while they sleep.

Melody spends the day with her research. She reads about the ghost of a Victorian doctor who threw himself out the window of room 333 after killing his new wife on their honeymoon. Now the doctor's ghost haunts the room above her, first appearing as a fluorescent orb of light that slowly takes shape of a man with arms outstretched, a dead gaze and no legs. Melody wonders how long the doctor must have been with his wife before he realized he'd been wasting so much time.

The rain patters against the window. Melody sets her computer on the bed and approaches the glass, staring deep at London's dreariness until she sees the reflection of her own gaze in the clouds.

You're a Melody.

Lewis' words used to sound so sincere but Melody has no idea what they mean now that the creaks above her are getting heavy. She hears the moans, the sounds of the couple upstairs fucking.

She looks up and swears she can feel the heat of Lewis' breath in her ear.

———

LOSING LEWIS used to be her biggest fear.

The fifth day is Melody's last in London. She packs her clothes and her toiletries. She makes the bed and cleans the room of her presence. She has no souvenirs except for the *I Love London* mug. She picks it off the desk and leaves all of Lewis' possessions behind.

The creaking above her continues, only this time it's a series of stomps that she can no longer ignore. Adrenaline builds inside of her as she pulls her luggage into the hall. She enters the elevator and waits until the doors slide closed. She touches the button on the panel and the elevator moans again, taking her up.

The air is cooler on the third floor. Its cold caress flushes Melody's cheeks. She clutches tight to the mug's ceramic handle and carries herself toward the haunted room. The gold numbers on the door glisten under the hallway light.

333

The door is propped ajar by the maid's cleaning cart. She pushes against its weight and a gush of frozen air slips from inside.

Neither of the maids notices Melody's presence. Their shadows shift in the bathroom. She recognizes the voices of the brunette and the redhead from her first morning in the hotel.

"They should board this room up, pretend it doesn't exist," the brunette says.

"Don't take this the wrong way," the redhead says, "but why do you even work here if you're so terrified of ghosts?"

The redhead sounds like Melody's sister, sounds like all the girls back home who knew better than Melody ever did.

"I love this hotel," the brunette says, her fondness echoing. "There's so much history here."

Melody presses in, her muscles working against the room's magnetic pull of energy. She holds her breath against the cold, her goosebumps like pinpricks that penetrate deep into her flesh, tickling her bones. The air thickens around her, tightens her limbs.

The maids don't notice as Melody meanders into the nightmare of the room. Discarded clothes lie scattered on the floor. Half-empty drinks wait to be finished on the nightstand. The bed's a mess, its mattress partially shifted off the box spring, almost as though something had shaken the two lovers from their passion. Sweat-stained sheets lie crumpled on the floor.

Chills brush over Melody's shoulder like a bony hand slipping over her skin, digging deep into her chest and squeezing her lungs. The foul taste of the coffee fills her mouth and trickles down her throat. The room's frigid air dries her eyes. She swallows and blinks, biting her tongue against the overwhelming sensation of her eyes being sucked inside of her head.

A creak echoes through her eardrums but there's nothing in the room. Melody's grasp tenses around the mug.

"Can you feel that?" the brunette asks, her voice a shaking from the bathroom.

"Feel what?" the redhead asks.

"Something's in here," the brunette shrieks.

Melody ignores the panic. She glances at the window, where Lewis' name is scrawled in her writing. She shakes her head. She blinks and the name is gone, replaced with a blank canvas of fogged glass.

You're a Melody.

She shudders, hearing a rustle against her ear. Her gaze locks on the window, on the droplets of water that form and trickle down. The dripping lines waver across the glass, slowly forming the crude shape of a bouquet of withered flowers.

CREDITS

All of the stories in this collection are reprinted with the permission of the author, except for "Grin on the Rocks," "Historical Hotties," "Modern Beasts," "Plot Points," and "Slippery Slopes," which are original stories, and are appearing here for the first time. "The Paper Bag Princess" originally appeared in *ManArchy* and was later reprinted in *Cease, Cows*. "Masturbating Megan's Strip Mall Exhibition" originally appeared in *Moonsick Magazine* under the title, "Masturbating Maggie's Strip Mall Exhibition." "Blue Hawaii" originally appeared in *Nova Parade* and was later reprinted in *The New Black*. "Cat Calls" originally appeared in *Exigencies*. "Tourist" originally appeared in *PANK*. "College Glaciers" originally appeared in *Punchnel's*. "Ghost Story" originally appeared in *Revolt Daily*. "Thinspiration" originally appeared in *Out of the Gutter*. "Better Places" originally appeared in *Pulp Modern* and was later reprinted in *Choose Wisely: 35 Women Up to No Good*.

ACKNOWLEDGMENTS

Thank you to everyone at The Writing Cult. While I've never actually met any of you in person, and our only interactions have been through the depths of the Internet, I've enjoyed getting to know you all over the years. I love reading your stories and seeing your daily adventures unfold on Facebook. Your companionship during all those late-nights spent procrastinating in lieu of writing has been more than comforting. You've made me a great writer. Here's to many more conversations about how great Steve Buscemi is.

REBECCA JONES-HOWE lives and writes in Kamloops, Canada. Her stories have appeared in *PANK*, *Punchnel's*, *Out of the Gutter* and *Pulp Modern*. She was the winner of *Lit Reactor*'s 2012 WAR writing competition. This is her first collection of short fiction. For more information visit her at http://rebeccajoneshowe.com/ or on Twitter at https://twitter.com/Rebnation.